Escape from Baxters' Barn

Escape from Baxters' Barn

WRITTEN & ILLUSTRATED BY

Rebecca Bond

HOUGHTON MIFFLIN HARCOURT
Boston   New York

www.hmhco.com

The text of this book is set in Brioso Pro.

The Library of Congress has cataloged the hardcover edition as follows:
Bond, Rebecca, 1972–
Escape from Baxters' Barn / by Rebecca Bond.
p. cm.
Summary: When Burdock, a young barn cat, sneaks into the house to get warm
he hears that the farmer, Dewey Baxter, has terrible plans that will endanger all
the animals, and he leads them in an attempt to escape before it is too late.
[1. Domestic animals—Fiction. 2. Adventure and adventurers—Fiction.
3. Farm life—Fiction.] I. Title.
PZ7.B63686Esc 2015
[Fic]—dc23
2014009053

ISBN: 978-0-544-33217-1 hardcover
ISBN: 978-1-328-74093-9 paperback

Manufactured in the United States of America
DOC 10 9 8 7 6 5 4 3 2 1
4500663275

For Cozette
—R.B.

Contents

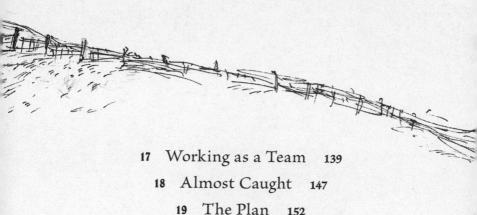

1

Ominous News

If Burdock had been obedient, the Baxter farmers' secret would have remained a secret.

Though it was only late September, the first cold crisp of autumn had slunk in overnight. It drifted down through the northern forests, tiptoed across the farm fields, and settled soundlessly into the old house and barn and disheveled outbuildings that made up the Baxter farm.

Burdock was having none of this cold.

In the barn, the gray tiger cat with large, moplike mitts and just one eye had awoken stiff and crabby from sleeping in a tight knot.

He decided to investigate the house for warmth.

This was his disobedience. For Burdock knew perfectly well he was strictly a barn cat. A *barn* cat, not a house cat, not even a sometimes-allowed-in-the-house barn cat. But Burdock loved warmth more than just about anything, and besides, he had no intention of getting caught.

Getting inside was easy enough to do.

Burdock slipped past the sleeping animals, steaming like teakettles, out the small hole in the barn doors into the early daylight. *Cold!* Quickly Burdock picked his way down the grassy path to the woodshed.

The woodshed, for winter convenience, was attached to the house and Burdock knew the shed's loft had a broken windowpane that let out onto the roof. In the dimness of morning, the cat silently climbed the stairs to the loft and maneuvered through the gap onto the patch-work of grayed roof shingles.

From here, he surveyed the farm for a moment.

The house was a faded yellow affair with a pitched roof and a covered porch on two sides. The old windows sat loosely and slightly askew in their casings, and the house's paint, especially on the west side, curled up in patches like birch bark. Behind the house was a small fenced-in vegetable garden. In front of the house, up a slight hill, were the barn and garage. And spreading out from that on three sides were pasturelands and hay fields, corn, and sunflowers.

Burdock looked beyond the open land, and

it seemed like only trees. All the way to the horizon a dense forest grew, mainly pine and fir, but stippled too with swaths of hardwood.

Ah, *there!* As Burdock turned his head he saw just what he had hoped to see — a ribbon of smoke coming up from the chimney. And now in his eagerness he wanted to run but he didn't dare; the roof was still slick with morning dew.

Burdock picked up his big paws and set them down carefully. One paw in front of the other, tail out for balance, like an apparition in the thin fog he crossed the ridgepole and reached the open upstairs bathroom window of the main house.

Quickly he hopped up to the sill, paused for a moment to listen, and dropped down onto the faded linoleum. He was in.

Oh warm! Inside, Burdock could smell the warmth before he felt it. He closed his one good eye, lifted his whiskered head, and sniffed: drying wool, bacon grease, and onions. And even on the landing at the top of the stairs, he could hear the gentle tick of the large cast-iron cookstove coming to life as it began to heat up. He crept down to the kitchen and curled into the toastiest spot.

As far back as he could remember, Burdock had never liked the cold. Born behind a post office to a stray mother cat, he was, unusually, the only kitten in the litter. Each night when his mother left to seek out food, Burdock burrowed into the newspapers in the old mail crate and tried to stay warm until she returned. Maybe if he'd had brothers or sisters it would have helped. It was hard to know. All he knew was that when he was wrapped in warmth, the world was put right.

BANG!

Burdock was yanked from blissful sleep under the stove. The shed door snapped open, cracked hard against the inside wall, boots pounded in, then the door banged shut.

Instantly alert, Burdock crouched, ears up, eye wide, and gaped at the slice of kitchen he could see through the narrow frame of stove and floor.

The door flew open again. Another pair of boots pounded in. Burdock froze.

"You're out of your *MIND*, Dewey!" yelled Grady. "You can't do this."

"Why not?" Dewey flung down his armload of firewood into the box beside the stove.

The terrific crash came so close, and was so surprisingly loud, Burdock instinctively leapt back. His claws scrabbled on the wood floor. Instantly he feared he'd be detected, but at the same time Dewey was shouting:

"Listen, Grady, what *else* are we gonna do? This farm is losing more money every single day and I don't see as *you've* had any bright ideas! What makes you so sure it's *not* gonna

work?" Dewey swung back a boot and angrily kicked a large chunk of kindling.

"Because it's completely *crazy*, Dewey! Could you just think a *little* here? This is a farm, for Pete's sake! You're a farmer, remember? You can't just —"

Already Dewey had turned, was stomping away.

"Dang it, Dewey, *listen!* You can't b —"

Dewey Baxter didn't stay to hear what his brother shouted after him. Dewey wrenched open the shed door again, slammed it shut from the other side, and gave it a violent kick for good measure.

But Burdock heard every word Grady said.

Hot as it was under the kitchen cookstove, the barn cat felt a shiver of ice.

2

Three Important Things

That evening, three important things happened at the same time.

1. Grady Baxter packed his bags, left a note on the kitchen table, and drove away from the farm.

2. The old mudroom radio broadcast plainly, "Storm advisory: Very heavy rains will be arriving Saturday from the southwest. Sustained gale-force winds expected across the listening region."

3. Burdock gathered the animals in the

barn and prepared to break the ominous news.

"What happened to *you?*" asked Figgy the pig. "Did you see a ghost?" Figgy's snout poked through the slats of her pen and her intelligent eyes appraised Burdock solemnly.

The barn cat was generally untended, with bits of hay, sticks, and burrs snarled in his bushy fur. Not to mention that with only one eye (the other had healed closed), he always looked slightly askew. But his current state went beyond his usual cockeyed appearance and questionable grooming. He looked genuinely spooked.

"I'll get to that," answered Burdock. "Uh, is everybody here? I've got some news."

Nanny, the cinnamon-colored goat, took initiative as usual. She too could tell by his expression that something was wrong. "Oh dear, Burdock. This doesn't look good. Let me help."

Nanny was a barn mother and liked to think

Three Important Things

that everyone could benefit from her crisp organization and kindly nature. She was good at it and beloved for it. But part of her wished she could be something grander than simply "Nanny." What kind of a name was *Nanny*? *Every* female goat was a nanny goat. Once she confided to Figgy the pig that she'd like to be called "Victoria or Valora or, best of all, *Gloria*." Something noble and brave. Figgy had laughed, lifted her snout in the air, and said, drawing out each syllable with precise and regal enunciation, "And *do* call me Queen Elizabeth!" and Nanny had laughed too.

Now Nanny hopped up on her hind legs, propped her front hooves on the middle rung of her pen, and peered over the top. As Burdock crouched down on the floor, Nanny gave him a concerned look, pausing for some moments to concentrate on him before she rallied everyone. It was unusual for everyone to come together like this, and Nanny wanted to do it properly.

"Okay everyone, let's gather round," announced the goat. "Burdock has something to say. I'll take roll. Figgy Piggy?"

"Nanny!" snorted Figgy. "Of course I'm here! I'm standing right —"

"Okay, all right," conceded Nanny. "Just going down the line. Fluff?"

"Oh, that's me!" said the sheep, who did truly look like a mound of white fluff with a face.

"Mrs. Brown?"

"Present," came the soft reply from Mrs. Brown. The old jersey milk cow lowered her huge, caramel eyes. A full barn meeting was unprecedented and made her nervous.

"All right, hon," said Nanny. "Pull?"

"Right here," came the molten voice of Pull, the enormous charcoal Shire draft horse. He shifted in his stall and swished at a fly with his tail.

"Tug?"

"As I live and breathe, I am here," echoed his equally massive brother. Tug's coat was dark brown, not as black, and his voice too was a shade lighter. And although both brothers weighed about the same (nearly two thousand pounds), Tug carried his tonnage with a hint of buoyancy and a twist of humor that Pull lacked.

"Tick?" asked Nanny.

"Here! Here I am!" Tick, Nanny's kid buck, bounced up and down. Tick was white with russet-brown dapples, a black nose, and ears that canted forward as if always listening. He sprung up with such vigor he threatened to topple Nanny over, so eager was he to see into the barn's central aisle and to hear about whatever the excitement was.

"With Burdock, that's seven. And I make eight," concluded Nanny. "We're all accounted for. Okay, Burdock, sugar, whatever you have to tell us, floor's yours."

Slowly Burdock stood up. Everyone waited for him to explain.

But now Burdock felt daunted. Except for young Tick, Burdock remained the newest inhabitant of the barn and he still wasn't sure what his place here was or, really, if he had a rightful place. Who was he to speak up? What's more, it was just such a staggering situation that he and the others were in. He couldn't quite think where to begin. But he had to tell them, didn't he?

"Go on, hon," Nanny coaxed gently, "what is it?"

"Thing is," Burdock started, "Dewey's planning — Grady was — What I'm trying to say is I overheard something" — his voice lowered to a whisper —"I heard a terrible thing."

Except for the old cow, Mrs. Brown, who took a step back, all the animals bent in just slightly closer.

Burdock glanced around at their intent faces.

"Spill, Burdock," said Figgy the pig.

"It seems," continued the cat, "that Dewey wants — that, that Dewey is — well, that Dewey intends to *burn down our barn*."

There, he had said it. Burdock looked down at the worn boards of the barn floor burnished dark with age. Although the cat wasn't much for aesthetics, right now the boards looked beautiful: all those whorls of pine grain, like rivulets of curling waves.

Burdock looked up. Everyone was staring at him.

"What?!" cried Figgy. "Wait! Start over!"

Figgy liked to get to the crux of things. She was a sharp thinker, a logical thinker, and this was illogical. Why would a farmer burn down his own barn?

"Now, from the beginning," she said.

So Burdock explained how he had snuck inside and gone to sleep under the stove. He told how Dewey and Grady had come into the house shouting. He repeated the brothers' argument as exactly as he could remember it. And he told how Dewey stormed out with Grady standing there yelling the terrible thing—*"You can't burn down the barn!"*—after him.

"Of course," said Burdock, "Grady didn't know I was there. After Dewey left, I peeked out, and Grady looked awful. Made me realize Grady knew his brother meant it."

Stunned, Nanny the goat opened her mouth to speak. It felt important to be reassuring, but she had no idea what to say.

"There's something more," Burdock said now.

"Oh boy," said Fluff the sheep, breathless. "This is exciting!"

Figgy rolled her eyes.

"I stayed under the stove for a while," continued Burdock. "I wanted to make sure I could get out without being seen, and just when it seemed all quiet I heard a car drive up and then a knock on the front door. I thought Dewey was outside, but he must have been in the den, because he came to the front and opened the door. From where I was, all I could see were Dewey's boots and another man's black shoes. The man with the shoes started to speak but Dewey yelled, 'Go away! Leave us alone already! Don't you have anything better to do?' I don't know where Grady was, but Dewey and this man argued awhile — it seemed to be about money, but I didn't really understand — Dewey talking really loud, the other man just calm-calm, like nothing could rile him up, until finally the man left but said he'd be back."

"Then what happened?" asked Figgy.

"That's what I'm getting to," said Burdock, easing himself back against a stall wall for support. "I heard Dewey say something to himself. He said, 'It's the only way out. The barn has to go.'"

"Mercy," whispered the old Mrs. Brown, picking up her dusty hooves and withdrawing farther into her stall. "It'll be the end of us!"

"Now, Mrs. Brown," said big Pull in his steady, solid way. "Keep your hair on. Let's think this through."

Burdock could never get over just how *big* Pull was, yet still the horse seemed to have a kind of gentleness about him.

"Could be Dewey is all mouth and no trousers," suggested Tug. "All vine and no taters."

"It makes no sense," said Nanny. "Does it, Figgy Piggy?"

"Mmmm," said Figgy. She seemed to be staring at nothing, considering.

"Dewey wouldn't," whispered Tick, who had followed every bit of this discussion with fascination and fear. "He wouldn't burn down the barn with us *in it*, would he, Mama?"

"Of course not," said Nanny quickly, not looking at Tick.

"You know," said Tug, "Dewey may be as sharp as marbles, but even so, why on earth would he burn down our barn?"

"He must have some reason for it," said Pull, considering.

Figgy looked across the aisle at Pull and the unfocused gaze of her eyes narrowed now to a fine point. She looked determined.

"I don't care what Dewey's harebrained reason is," she said, "the important thing to keep in mind is us. We can only assume we are running out of time."

"Yes, we need to grab this nettle," said Tug.

"Which means what?" asked Nanny.

"It means we need to take action; we need a plan," translated Pull.

"Oh, then yes. Precisely," said Nanny, mustering more confidence than she felt. "We need a plan."

And so it was agreed among the barn animals that each would do some hard thinking, and they all would reassemble the next evening, same time, same place, with ideas.

Later that night, as the wind tore leaves off the maples in the valley and the animals hunched in their pens listening, a creamy white form sailed down from the barn rafters, banked a perfect right turn, and glided soundlessly out the side window into the blackening sky.

3

A Talk with Pull

Sleep was one of the few things Burdock excelled at, but last night he had hardly slept at all.

Partly this was because he felt more than a little angry with Dewey.

Partly Burdock felt aggravated by the restless churning of the other animals, their pacing hooves pervading the barn long after it was usually claimed by silence.

But on top of all that? This miserable cold! In the coldest months Burdock dreamed of being a house cat.

Burdock had never really been a house cat, not for long. His brief kittenhood in the mail crate ended abruptly one day when his mother simply didn't return. At least it had been almost summer and he could set out on his own to look for food and shelter wherever he could find it. It hadn't been easy. Finally, in the late fall, with the days again turning brisk, Burdock thought everything was going to change when he was discovered by a young man who carried him home to his wife. They had radiant heat and soft, woolly beds, but they also had a big dog, a new baby, and a small house, so it wasn't long before Burdock was passed on to another house down the street where the man knew there were several cats already. Too many, really. The next spring Burdock was unceremoniously dropped off by the mailboxes at the Baxter farm.

To Burdock it had felt like he was a pair of boots that didn't fit anyone.

Now a year and a half later, in the chilly blue of early morning, the gray cat stepped out of Baxters' barn. He threaded through the tall grass fringing the building and carefully arranged himself on one of the discarded tires heaped along the pasture fence. Burdock knew the tires would catch the first morning sun and their black skin would heat up nicely. He settled his chin on his large paws and closed his eye.

If sleeping — and disappearing — were Burdock's goals, he didn't achieve either. Before long the animals were let out to pasture and soon the big draft horse Pull crunched nearby on his jumbo-size feet. Then he saw Burdock.

The horse had never paid special attention to the solitary cat, but things were different now, so when he spied Burdock lying in the sun, he wanted to talk.

"Burdock," he intoned, his voice dark and smooth. "How are you doing?"

Burdock lifted his head to answer when he

caught sight of Dewey rounding the corner of the barn.

"Look," he whispered.

Pull turned and together their steady gazes followed the man as he moved up the hill to where a few old apple trees crowned the slope. Here Dewey stopped and looked down on the farm as if appraising the place.

"What do you think he has in mind?" asked Pull.

"What do you mean? We *know* what he has in mind, don't we?" answered the cat.

"I mean, do you think he has a plan worked out already? Do you think Dewey's been thinking about this for a long time?"

Burdock raised a whiskered eyebrow. "I don't know. Does it matter? What are you getting at?"

"I'm just saying people can surprise you," sighed Pull. "Listen, I'm sure I've never told you this, but before Tug and I came here we worked on another farm. It was a big place and we worked under a hired man named Hal. He was very capable, and kind to us, and we really liked him. *Everybody* liked him. We felt lucky. So we were as surprised as anyone when Hal ended up pocketing the money he was supposed to be spending on expensive veterinary medicines. The farm only figured it out when a few animals died."

Pull's remembering face was sad. It was strange for Burdock to see enormous Pull looking forlorn.

"And, as it turned out," Pull continued, "Hal had been stealing for a long time. That's what made me the angriest. All that time we thought he was our friend and I had grown to trust him." Pull snorted a disparaging blast of air through his nose. "It's a very strange thing to lose trust in someone you had faith in. You just want to believe your friends are on your side."

Burdock wasn't used to thinking about things like this. He hadn't really had friends or family to rely on and trust. But everything Pull said made sense.

"What about Dewey?" Burdock asked. "Do you trust him?"

Pull's eyes met Burdock's. "Dewey has never felt like a friend. Trust him? No. Though really, after what happened with Hal, I'm not sure I'm ready to trust anyone."

Burdock regarded the horse. The cat felt vaguely honored that Pull talked to him openly like this.

Burdock and Pull looked back up the hill at the figure in the trees. Dewey was shaking the branches forcefully, jerking the gnarled limbs back, and letting them go with a snap. With one final terrific jolt, there was a moment of still silence before a salvo of apples came thundering down like stones.

4

Fluff's Escape

A big storm was coming.

By four o'clock that afternoon, the first beads of rain had started to fall, and most people had made their last preparations and were heading inside.

"Batten down the hatches," Noreen Claussen, the town clerk, called gaily as she screwed her gas tank cap back on at Gus's Gas. She had a new roof, and she liked a good storm.

Mrs. Frisk, who lived over the post office, hummed as she made a lemon meringue pie.

Jeff Townes, who ran the auto parts store,

sat in his favorite chair, reading the newspaper, and watched the weather channel.

Rosie Carmine worked on her wedding dress, delighted to be home early.

There was nothing more to do but tuck up inside and await the tempest that was forecast to gather strength through the night and hit peak force tomorrow, Saturday, in the evening.

As Dewey was herding the animals back into the barn for the night, walking behind them on the short stretch of road and hollering whenever anyone strayed to nibble the long grass, Fluff the sheep made a break for it.

Burdock was the only one who didn't witness it. He was in the back garden under a rosebush.

But all the other animals watched.

"Baaa!" Fluff bleated, bolting down the embankment and racing across the grass. It hardly seemed she had her eyes open, the way she bar-

reled through a shrub and tumbled into a ditch. And still, after righting herself, she went headlong through the laundry, unwittingly pulling down clothes, snapping off clothespins, even somehow managing to festoon herself with a pair of Dewey's long underwear. Until, without a break in her stride, she hotfooted around the corner of the house and was gone. The last

Dewey saw of her was her heels kicking up and several divots of lawn flying away.

"Oh, *a rat's behind!*" Dewey yelled now. "Where the devil is she *going?!*"

Figgy glanced at Nanny and let out a snort. Tick giggled. Even the big horses looked entertained.

"No one can accuse her of piddle-diddling," whispered Tug appreciatively. "She's taking *action.*"

But Dewey was not pleased. He hastily corralled the other animals into the barn. Then he went after Fluff.

Under the rosebush, hidden from outside view, Burdock was in his favorite hideaway. He was making a rare attempt at grooming when a flash of white went galloping jauntily by. Then Dewey thundered past.

Burdock wasn't sure what to make of the situation. Was everyone just fleeing? Had it come to that? No, this seemed more like one of Fluff's impromptu endeavors, for which she was well known. Still, Burdock wondered briefly if she might actually get away.

He peered out between the rose branches and watched.

Despite the piles of sausage and potatoes he ate, Dewey was fast. Steadily he closed the distance between himself and the sheep and when he was close enough he launched himself forward like the football player he had once been, tackling Fluff and dropping her to the ground.

"BAAA!" she bleated indignantly, but Dewey wasn't letting go.

Without much gentleness, he dragged Fluff back to the barn. He grabbed fistfuls of wool and simply yanked her along. The sheep's feet scrabbled in the dirt to keep up.

Burdock crept behind them to the barn, thinking Dewey seemed more volatile than ever.

"Now, that was lively!" said Figgy, after Dewey had penned Fluff, stormed out, and slammed the doors.

"It just sort of happened," panted the sheep. She took a long drink of water from her pail and shrugged. "I saw the barn doors and I was suddenly afraid to go back in. I hadn't really thought it through."

"Oh no?" said Figgy.

"Don't tease her, Figgy," Nanny said and glowered at the pig. Figgy pretended not to see.

"Okay," called Nanny, "meeting's in ten minutes!"

5

How Can We Get Out?

"So what all do you think?" asked Nanny. "Let's hear everyone's ideas."

It was early evening. The rain coming down made a gentle pattering on the tin roof. The animals had reassembled and roll had been called. Inside, the barn had the nice earthy smell of sweet hay, musky horse, molasses oats, and wood.

On the left side of the barn's central aisle were the pens of Mrs. Brown and Pull and Tug, their heads and shoulders visible above the stalls' half doors. On the right side was Nanny and Tick's pen, next to that, Figgy's, and then Fluff's.

Burdock perched on a coil of ragged rope that lay discarded in the wide central aisle of the barn.

"Thoughts, anyone?" said Nanny again.

No one said anything.

Burdock glanced to the left and the right as best as he could without moving. He didn't like being seated where everyone could focus on him. It made him feel as if more than his presence was required, as if he would be expected to actually talk, and he hadn't thought of one intelligent thing to say.

Except for the rain, it was quiet in the barn.

Pull shifted his ponderous weight in the straw, breaking the stillness.

"Well," said Nanny.

Even though it wasn't yet night, the barn lay in darkness under the approaching storm's gray coat.

"The way I see it," ventured Pull, clearing his throat and beginning slowly in his deep, grainy voice, "is since we don't know for certain what Dewey's plan is, we need a plan ourselves — an escape plan."

"Oh, Pull, good idea!" said Fluff admiringly.

"Oh please," snorted Figgy. "We all know that much."

"What I mean is," said Pull, "we need a way to get out of the barn. We're all closed in our stalls at night and the barn doors are locked."

Locked? wondered Burdock. He had never realized this.

"Really?" asked Nanny. "How do you know that?"

"You can hear it," said Pull. "Every evening, when Dewey leaves, he closes the doors, right? And first you hear that horrible creaking he never fixes, and then you hear a *clunk*, like some heavy kind of — well — board, or brace, is being dropped into place."

"Hmm . . ." said Nanny, thinking. She turned

to Burdock. "Burdock, love, I know it's wet out, but might you go check please?"

Burdock picked himself up from the coil of rope, made his way down the aisle, and slipped out the small, jagged hole in the door. With the rain coming down more thickly now, he crouched under the overhang of the roof and peered up.

Of course Burdock had seen the doors many times before, but he had never really *looked* at them. Sure enough, a heavy oak bar slotted down into two L-shaped grips, one on each of the tall wooden doors, locking the animals inside.

Burdock returned through the small hole and settled back down on the pile of rope. "Just as Pull said," he confirmed, then gave a full description.

"Well, if that's not grist for the mill," said Tug.

"It's certainly not good," sighed Nanny.

"I just hope," said Mrs. Brown in a near whisper, lifting her head up above her stall door,

Escape from Baxters' Barn

"that we can get out before Dewey"— her voice became nearly inaudible —"does what he's intending to do."

"Agreed," said Pull. "But hope is not a plan. We need to think. I say we get cracking. I've liked it here well enough until now — though I will say the feed seems not to be as good quality lately —"

"Or as plentiful," added Tug.

"Or as plentiful," agreed Pull. "But everything's different now. Yesterday morning, Burdock heard Dewey say, 'It has to be the barn,' which sounds to me like his mind is made up. And I would say Grady is the smarter one here — certainly more level-headed — and might be able to stop Dewey, but has anyone seen Grady since yesterday?"

"The truck is gone," said Figgy.

"Right," emphasized Pull. "It's been gone *since yesterday.* Grady *never* goes away overnight. Have you ever known Grady to not be here for even a night?" Several animals shook their heads. Burdock tried to remember if he'd seen Grady since the kitchen argument, and decided he hadn't.

"It seems pretty obvious to me," continued Pull. "Dewey is going to burn down the barn. It's likely he is planning to take us down with it. And let's be straight: I, for one, have no intention of *dying* here."

It was a chilling thought that silenced everyone.

On the roof, the rain continued to drum steadily and the constant patter high above the animals' heads reinforced the very outline of their home.

Burdock looked up into the darkness at the beams of the high peak. Until now this structure had always seemed like such a thoroughly permanent thing.

"So, then, how do we get out?" asked Nanny.

"We could try to leave during the day," suggested Tug.

"I thought of that," said Figgy, "but first, as you know, all the pastures have mighty powerful electric fences. Second, if Dewey did catch us trying to escape, he'd find us and haul us back, and who *knows* what he'd do then, and so third, I think we need to escape when Dewey couldn't possibly think it. He's always mucking around during the day. We have to just vanish in the dark so he'll never know we're gone."

"Vanish?" asked Fluff, incredulous.

"*Escape,*" said Figgy irritably, "I mean escape."

"But how can we get out?" Nanny asked again.

"Well, yes," agreed Pull. "That's the big question."

The meeting ended with no clear plan. As soon as the gathering was over, Burdock slipped away up the corner staircase to the hayloft. He didn't usually come up here — the air here was gritty with hay dust — but with the rain battering down he wasn't going outside, and he wanted to be someplace where he could be alone and undisturbed.

He had an odd feeling fizzing on the edges of his brain and as he tucked into a pocket between two hay bales he let himself think it: *he could escape.*

It was dumb, Burdock knew, that he hadn't thought of this before. But the truth was it had taken Nanny asking him to go out and check the doors for him to realize it: unlike the others, *he* was not trapped in a stall or locked in by the barn doors. Nothing really was preventing him from walking away from Dewey, the barn, his life here with the other animals. Burdock the cat could go it alone.

6

Nanny

As predicted, rain pelted down in torrents through the night, pounding like thousands of hammers on the roof, cascading in sheets off the edges. On the ground, all around the periphery of the barn, water smacked down with such force it carved out trenches, which filled with more water, which only amplified the sound of more rain bucketing down.

At six the next morning, when the sky usually would have started to lighten, it remained dark as charcoal. The storm was really just beginning. The full brunt of it was still forecast for tonight.

Burdock awakened and made a few exploratory stretches. He was hungry. He would go
to the feed room — sometimes he caught mice
there.

As he descended the narrow corner stairs,
Burdock suddenly heard on top of the steady
rain a series of unfamiliar sounds: a scrabble, a

few clunks, and an abrupt loud *thump*. Then, "Oof!"

What on earth? Burdock crept down the remaining stairs and angled his whiskered head cautiously around the corner.

"Nanny!" he gasped, spying the goat standing proudly, if a bit shaken-looking, in the central aisle. "How did you get out of your pen?"

"I jumped!" answered Nanny, giving her body a good wriggle back and forth. Bits of hay and dust drifted down from her coat.

In the night, Nanny had had a thought. *I'm a goat,* she thought. It may not seem like much of a revelation, but in a way it was.

Until now, Nanny didn't do all the naughty things that goats elsewhere are notoriously known to do. She didn't chew the bumpers off cars or munch through tin siding like it was lettuce, she didn't bash posts with her powerful horns, and she didn't jump fences. But she *was* a goat. And goats can jump.

"You jumped?" asked Mrs. Brown, who was

awake now too and looking in wonderment over her stall. "That must have been the small earthquake I just felt."

"I crashed into your wall," said Nanny.

"What's going on?" came the sleepy voice of Figgy. Her pink snout pushed through her pen's cracks. "Whoa! Nanny! Look at you. How'd you get out there?"

"I jumped," said Nanny again. If you were looking for it, you would have seen just a slight raising of her tufted chin.

"How *unruly*, Nanny!" exclaimed Figgy with real appreciation.

"Here," said Nanny. "I think I can do it again. Let me show you."

Burdock stepped to the side, well out of the way as Nanny backed up to Mrs. Brown's stall, ran a few steps, and sprung up over her pen wall. Just for a moment Burdock thought she wouldn't clear it, but only Nanny's hoofs clacked on the top rail and she landed successfully, albeit with a thud, in the hay.

"Mama!" came Tick's voice. Then a laugh.

In a moment, Nanny was back in the central aisle, striking the boards of Mrs. Brown's stall.

"Very graceful," said Figgy. "Well done!"

By now the horses and Fluff were awake too.

"No way!" exclaimed Fluff. "Let's *all* do that!"

Before the others could explain that sheep are not springy like goats, there was a scrabble of hooves and Fluff's expectant face appeared briefly above her pen's edge. Burdock could tell she really thought she was going to make it.

She didn't. There was a crash, followed by a dull but significant crunch in the hay; it sounded like a bag of feed had been dropped from a not inconsequential height.

"Ooooch," came a faint voice from the depths of the straw.

"Oh dear, you okay in there, hon?" asked Nanny, moving forward to peer into Fluff's pen.

"Just fine!" called Fluff gaily.

Figgy snorted. Tug chuckled. And Tick bobbed up and down, up and down, finally falling back in the hay and giggling a bright, bubbling laugh. He hadn't really laughed in a few days, and it felt good.

"Fools rush in!" exclaimed Tug.

Suddenly, Burdock noticed something. The latch on each pen, he saw now, was nothing more than a big rectangular block of wood, nailed straight through the middle with one strong spike. Turn the block horizontally, and the gate wouldn't budge. But turn the block *vertically*, and the gate could easily be pushed open.

The block latch on Figgy's gate, for example, looked like this:

"Wow," breathed Burdock.

"Wow, what?" asked Figgy.

"I see how Nanny might be able to get you all out," answered Burdock.

He pointed out the blocks to her.

"Couldn't *you* turn those?" he asked. Nanny stared at them for a few moments.

"I see what you mean," she said.

As everyone watched, Nanny walked around so that her body was parallel to the wall that fronted the pens. She took a few steps, bucked up with her hind legs, and lightly butted underneath Figgy's block latch. The block rotated fully upright and then continued to turn more, like the hand of a clock moving backwards from its original position at three, to vertical twelve, back a smidge farther to eleven. Nanny had knocked it just a touch too hard, swinging it past the open vertical position, again to locked.

"Try from the other side," offered Burdock

Nanny came around to the other side of the

block and repeated her efforts, only now she tapped the block ever so slightly. It pivoted to the right a notch and rested, perfectly upright.

"Push, Figgy!" she exclaimed. "Push your gate!"

Figgy did. The gate swung easily open, and Figgy dashed out into the wide open aisle too. She spun in a circle, reveling in the unexpected freedom of it.

Nanny had gotten her out!

"I'll be darned!" said Pull, leaning forward.

"Far out!" exclaimed Fluff.

"You're a bright spark, Burdock!" said Tug. "And you're a Jack-be-nimble, Nanny!"

"If that doesn't beat all!" said Figgy, drawing

out each word and looking at first Burdock and then Nanny in a way she never had before.

Burdock sat back on his haunches, enjoying the feeling.

Under the pressure of a terrible situation, the barn animals were turning out to be thinkers *and* doers.

7

Dreams

The piercing, rusty creak of the barn doors could be heard clearly above the rain.

"Dewey!" whispered Figgy.

In a flash, the pig trotted back into her pen. Nanny nudged Figgy's gate closed, but there wasn't time to turn the block latch before she hurdled over the fence into her own pen. As she did this, Burdock scurried around the far corner, the raggedy brush of his tail disappearing just as an unshaven Dewey appeared.

In the gloom of the stormy morning, Dewey loomed large. He clomped down the aisle with a three-legged stool tucked under his arm, milk pail in one hand, a glistening hunk of sausage in the other. He opened Mrs. Brown's stall and let her out into the aisle. Stuffing the remainder of the meat into his mouth and chewing, he sat down on the stool to milk Mrs. Brown.

It was only after, as Dewey was grouching about the increasingly foul weather and hurriedly feeding the animals since it was too wet to put them out to pasture, that he noticed the block latch on Figgy's pen.

"Huh," he grunted, staring. "Must of forgot to close that one. Course, *you* didn't notice." He looked Figgy in the eye. "Could have been out with your nose in the feed all night, having yourself a fine feast, if only you had a noodle in your noggin!"

Dewey spent the morning in the garage attached to the back of the barn.

The garage had once housed the Baxter brothers' second tractor, but that had been sold long ago. Now it housed Dewey's baby — an antique car, inherited from his uncle.

It was a 1930 baby blue Ford Model A roadster. Splendidly outfitted with a four-cylinder, two-liter engine, a three-speed gearbox, and state of the art brake design, its mechanics were top-notch.

While Grady had often tried to convince Dewey to sell his heirloom automobile when the brothers started to slide on their bills, Dewey would not hear of it. He was forever hunting down parts for his "Baby Blue," and his dream was to restore the car to her original glory as closely as possible.

Today, Dewey pulled the overhead cord to illuminate the garage, switched on the ancient radio that sat on the upper shelf, and did a little tidying. It was a rare thing to see Dewey organizing, but he busily began boxing up his piles of tools, automotive parts, and garage equipment.

Meanwhile, lying on a pile of empty grain sacks in the feed room, Burdock thought about cream. In his opinion, he didn't get nearly enough. Occasionally Grady had given him a straight-from-the-cow warm dish of it, but never as often as Burdock would like. And with Dewey in charge now, Burdock doubted there was cream in his future.

Under the rhythmic tumble of water on the roof, Burdock's mind drifted. Thoughts of warm cream led to images of warm sun, then woolly beds, cozy stoves, and cooking pots whose bubbling chicken juices perfumed the air.

Burdock's mouth watered, and now he pictured himself in a kitchen on a thick, braided rug next to a wood stove. It was not so unlike the Baxters' cookstove, but here Burdock was not squirreled away beneath it, hiding. Here, he was out in the open, basking in the warmth, in the freedom of belonging. Here, he had just finished a bowl of moist chicken parts and was meticulously licking his whiskers clean before curling up to sleep.

The vision was so real, so right, that Burdock would have willed himself there if he could have. Far away from this damp, doomed barn.

8

Figgy

While Burdock slept, Figgy was thinking.

Contrary to what Dewey had said, Figgy did have a noodle in her noggin. Her mind worked like a puzzle, fitting pieces into place until a whole picture emerged.

After snuffling about in her trough for any last scrap of potato peel, bread crust, or tangy cheese rind, Figgy lay down, closed her eyes, and let out a sigh. The howl of the wind was louder now, and the rain hitting the barn was heavier. The deluge of water crashed into the building in waves as fierce squalls drove the storm sideways.

Figgy stretched herself out. Some of her best thinking came while lying down. She thought about what she knew:

1. Nanny can get out of her own pen.
2. Nanny can get us out of our pens.
3. The barn doors are locked.
4. The only one who can get outside is Burdock.
5. There's no way Burdock can open the barn doors.

There were some good and some bad things here. The sticking point of any escape plan, it seemed, was getting out of the barn — or, in other words, finding a way to open the locked doors. Figgy's mind went back over exactly how Burdock had described the wooden bar. Clearly, Burdock wasn't big enough or strong enough to lift it and open the doors.

But wait, what about Nanny? Could she push the bar up and open the doors? Despite her kind, motherly demeanor, Nanny was strong. And clever. Hadn't she just jumped the fence and turned the block on Figgy's pen by butting it with her head? *What if* — Figgy started to sit up — *Rats!* she remembered, *Nanny's locked in too.*

So here was the real question: How could Nanny get out of the barn and at least try to open the doors for the rest of them? She wasn't that big, really. Could she squeeze through anywhere? Was there any, any way?

There was the door to the garage, but Dewey always kept that locked. The barn had a couple of decent-size windows, but they were so high up on the walls, even Tug and Pull couldn't see out of them. And — well, that was it. Figgy tried to think if there were any gaps between or under the outside boards. She couldn't remember having seen any. Figgy opened her eyes and looked at her own outside barn wall.

The Baxter barn had been built over a hundred years ago, in 1892. It was simply one big space with a half loft, intended as a holdall for animals, equipment, and hay. There was no foundation and originally, simply a dirt floor. Sometime in the early 1930s, a floor had been added to most of the barn, all except the sheep, goat, and pig pens, which ran along the west side and remained dirt.

The barn was well built and had stayed in good shape, with only minor repairs now and then. Five years ago, when an old maple tree fell on the barn and an expensive new roof was needed, Grady convinced Dewey that they needed to take out some insurance on the structure. Dewey grumbled but finally agreed. They were already so deep in the hole, really, so what the heck?

Figgy looked at a small puddle of water seeping under the wall.

Suddenly she was on her feet, pawing at the puddle. A little chunk of sandy mud came up. Quickly, she pawed with both front hooves, scraping back the water and the dirt. The hard-

packed earth had been softened some by the
soaking rain. Figgy pushed her snout in and
carved out a groove. She dug furiously with her
hooves, scraping back an inch of dirt, then an
inch more. A jolt of energy surged through her.
She clawed harder, deepening the hollow at the
base of the wall. She poked her nose in again
and pried up. Dug more. Pulled back the dirt
and stopped. *Wow*, thought the pig. This might
work.

"*Nanny,*" whispered Figgy.

9

A Plan Takes Shape

Dewey wasn't really listening to the radio. But when the broadcast was interrupted by three loud beeps, he put down the box of waxes and polishes, went over to the radio, and turned up the volume.

EMERGENCY ALERT. HURRICANE-FORCE WINDS MOVING RAPIDLY INTO THE LISTENING AREA. WINDS GUSTING TO EIGHTY MILES PER HOUR. DAMAGING CONDITIONS IN EFFECT THROUGH SUNDAY MORNING. SEEK IMMEDIATE SHELTER.

"Oh, *ROT!*" cried Dewey. He burst through

the garage door, ran down the barn aisle and out the front doors, slammed and barred them, and raced up the road.

The rain coming down now was torrential but he didn't even stop for a coat.

"Pssst! Sleepyhead!" Nanny called out to Burdock. With Dewey gone, Nanny had quickly gathered the group for a meeting. Everyone was there except for Burdock, who was in the feed room on top of a box of grain sacks. By leaning her head over her pen's edge, Nanny could glimpse just a ruffle of gray fur slowly rising and falling.

Except for his slow, even breathing, Burdock didn't move an inch.

"Burdock!" called Nanny again. "Burdock, love!" There was excitement in Nanny's voice. "*BURRR-DOCK!*"

"What? Where?" Burdock awoke with a start, flipping over to face the disturbance, his one eye opening wide. "Is the barn on fire?"

"Oh, no dear," said Nanny. "We're having a meeting. We need you."

Burdock flopped back onto his side, stretched out his gray arms, and languidly kneaded the air with his broad mitteny paws. "I was dreaming about chickens . . ." His voice trailed off and he yawned again, his tongue unfurling like a glossy pink ribbon. "Don't any of you ever sleep?" He closed his eye, pulled his paws up under his chin, and turned over.

But Nanny urged him again. And soon, Burdock arrived and settled himself on his coil of rope. His sour expression and crumpled whiskers said he was bristling slightly to be awake. But in truth, Burdock was curious. What was going on now?

"Before Dewey gets back," said Nanny, "let's talk. Shall I call roll?"

"We're all here!" exclaimed Figgy. "Just talk!"

Nanny hadn't dared to jump into the central aisle in case Dewey should suddenly reappear, so she was again standing with her front hooves propped on the middle board of her pen. The other animals gathered around as best they could.

"Figgy believes," began Nanny, "that she can dig a tunnel under her wall to the outside. Big enough for me to fit through. She's already started to dig and it seems possible. Right, Figgy?" Nanny looked to Figgy.

"As far as I can figure," explained Figgy, "it's the only way out. And I think it could work."

As she began to talk, Burdock noticed a glister in Figgy's eyes, the kind you get when you have latched on to a major idea, or a major idea has latched on to you.

"And if she can get *me* out," continued Nanny, "the hope is that I can knock that big bar off the barn doors. Unlock them." She paused. Nanny was far from sure she really could do this, but what other chance did they have? "And then I can open your stalls, and we can all get out."

"I'll say!" said Tug. "Aren't you a clever clog!"

"There's one thing," said Figgy, jumping in. "If I dig out all that dirt, we need somewhere to *put* it, some way to hide it. Because of course Dewey will notice if my pen suddenly fills up with a great mound of dirt ... but I think I can push some of it to you, Fluff, under our shared wall, and some of it to you, Nanny and Tick, under our wall, and can you distribute it around your pens? You know, spread it about under the straw to get rid of it?"

"Yes, yes!" cried Tick exuberantly. "I can help! I can do that! Can't I, Mama?" He bounded lightly up and down on his little black feet.

"That would be an enormous help, love," said Nanny with a nod.

Unable to contain himself, Tick gamboled a few enthusiastic laps around the pen.

"And Fluff, you on board?" asked Figgy.

"Absolutely!" said Fluff. "My wish is your command!"

"Uh, don't you mean ... well, point taken," said Figgy.

"How long do you think it will take you?" asked Mrs. Brown quietly.

"I don't know," said Figgy. "A day or two? I will say this: as dreary as all this rain is, we should at least be grateful that Dewey can't burn down the barn when it's this wet."

"Absolutely true," said Pull. "At least it's giving us a little time. But wait—" He paused as a thought came to him. Leaning forward, he asked, "Won't Dewey see the hole?"

"Not if I can help it," explained the pig matter-of-factly. "I'm going to cover it with hay when I'm not digging. Easy-peasy." She looked pleased. Just as much as Figgy loved a chunk of buttermilk cornbread or a dollop of beans baked with maple syrup, the pig could appreciate a well-designed strategy.

"Marvelous," said Pull. "We have a plan." Cautious relief could be heard seeping into his voice. "An escape plan."

The wind bashed the barn suddenly and the whole structure trembled. It made the animals feel momentarily unmoored.

"But, Mama," came the small voice of Tick, "if we *can* get out, then, where will we all — *go?*" Tick didn't think he was asking a big question. He was young enough to assume that his elders had that part figured out.

But none of them (except maybe Burdock if you count his dreaming) had even let themselves imagine that far.

Fluff was lying in her pen nervously listening to the relentless pummeling of wind, when she saw a ghost. It swooped down through the murky dark at the top of the barn and hovered for a moment, not even ten feet above her head.

"Help!" she bleated. "Help! Figgy, *look!*"

Figgy was digging at the hole, snout and hooves scraping and gouging, but at Fluff's cry, she turned and looked up just as a white, feathery shape glided a silent half circle, flickered out the window, and was gone.

"Oh!" Figgy breathed, her voice hushed with awe. "A barn owl!"

"I've never seen an owl in this barn," whispered Mrs. Brown, who had been listening. "There's an owl here?"

"Apparently," said Figgy, "there was. Though why he would go out in weather like this, I haven't the foggiest idea."

10

Fear

The wind that night was a thrashing wind, a bellowing wind, a prying wind. It battered trees, blasted through glass, and ripped away anything it could get its grip on. Burdock crawled under a cabinet in the tool room and took note of every appalling noise.

And the tempest wasn't just at the Baxter farm.

In town, in the middle of the night, the gazebo on the village green was wrenched loose from its wooden base and tumbled down the hill to lean affectionately against the information booth.

In the morning, the swings at the elementary school were found wrapped tightly around and around the top bar, as if by a troublesome child.

And Mr. and Mrs. Cavanaugh's wrought iron bench disappeared off their front porch, only to be discovered upright in their garden, on the other side of the house. "Oh, I like it there," said Mrs. Cavanaugh. "It's poetic."

In the Baxter farm kitchen, Dewey slammed around.

Early this morning, he had run down the road to check again on the crop of sunflowers. The fields of towering flowers had been only days away from harvest, and Dewey had been counting on this crop to pull him through the year financially.

It had been somewhat of a gamble to plant sunflowers in the first place, especially this far north, but the brothers had been told that the market for sunflower oil was growing. They were led to believe that if they could turn a decent harvest, there would be a sizeable profit.

But any earnings were all gone now. The storm had taken care of that.

In the fields, sunflower stalks lay strewn about like giant matchsticks. Overnight, the entire crop had been devastated.

Dewey was steamed.

"This *PLACE!*" he bellowed at the empty kitchen, kicking the leg of an old dresser and catapulting dishes to the floor.

Darn Grady for leaving! Darn him for getting out. Dewey kicked a fallen jar and stood there, practically snarling in his anger. Maybe he should do the same thing: leave this joint. But then he would need a chunk of cash to get started doing something else.

Dewey laid his palms down on the counter, thinking back over his arguments with Grady and with the man who had come just after to collect their money.

"Well, Grady, I don't know where you are!" yelled Dewey, "but *I'm* calling the shots now!"

Digging was much harder than Figgy had hoped. And exhausting. Last night, as midnight came and midnight went, she had raked at the dirt with her hooves and levered with her snout, but still she hadn't broken through. She stepped back to survey her progress. *This was a dumb idea,* she thought to herself. *You can't just tunnel through a hundred-year-old floor!* She hated that she had let everyone believe she could do this.

All she wanted to do now was stop, push the hay into a big, soft mountain, and throw herself down on it. She took a step toward her bed, could feel its magnetic pull. How wonderful it would be to flop down, lay her head gratefully to the ground, rustle her body around until it felt just right . . . As she thought about it she let herself relax. She bent her knees, readying to give in. *Sleep.*

But something, the tiniest spark of something, pulled her back, snapped her to attention. Maybe it was a small snore from Fluff, or maybe Tick mumbled in his sleep. "No, Figgy," she said to herself, straightening. She furrowed her brow and scowled sternly into the dark. "To destroy our chance by just *giving up* would be despicable." She had volunteered herself for this task and as nearly impossible as it now seemed, the others were depending on her.

And so, through the long night, to the rhythm of the rain, from one a.m. to two, two to three, three to four and on to five, a weary but resolved pig dug and dug and dug and dug.

By early morning, when the barn at last stopped shuddering, the torrent on the roof slowed to a trickle, and a ray of early dawn red brightened the east windows, an achy, dirty, and thoroughly worn-out Figgy finally fell gratefully asleep.

The horrible creak of the doors announced Dewey's arrival. Figgy jerked awake.

"Oh no! *The dirt!*" she cried. There was a real pile of it now that hadn't yet been dispersed.

In a quick second, Figgy scrambled onto her hooves and attacked the mound, kicking frantically at the dirt, nosing it under the hay, pushing it toward the edges of her pen, and tromping madly to flatten it down.

Immediately Nanny saw what was happening.

"*Burdock!*" she hissed.

The cat had just emerged from under the tool cabinet and was in the aisle, groggily stretching out his hind legs one after the other. He stepped now to the side to make room for Dewey when Nanny whispered, "*Burdock! Stall him!*"

It took a moment for Burdock to catch on, but he did, just as Dewey was passing, almost to the pig's pen.

The cat sprang out in front of Dewey and

clipped him at the ankles. Dewey stumbled, caught himself with a hand on Nanny's pen, turned, and cursed.

"Blast it, Burdock! What's wrong with you?" Dewey gave the cat a rough shove with his boot, knocking Burdock into the pen wall.

Figgy didn't have a moment's more time. The dirt was mostly gone but *the hole!* She dove against the wall, covering the small pit with her bulk, and squeezed shut her eyes. *Look relaxed,* Figgy commanded herself.

"Well, don't *we* look comfortable!" chided Dewey as he righted himself and clomped by.

Figgy let out a lungful of air.

"Are you all right, love?" whispered Nanny to Burdock. She looked through her pen's slats at the cat.

"I think so," said Burdock, shaking his head slowly. "He's never done that before."

"I know," said Nanny. She paused. "I don't know what would've happened if Dewey had seen the hole. Thank you for doing that, Burdock."

Burdock stood for a moment looking up at Nanny. Lately, she had been demanding things of him, but she was kind. Just the way she looked at him made him feel she cared about him.

"Why don't you come lie down in here for a while," offered Nanny now. "Tick and I would be happy for your company."

Burdock hesitated, but when Tick stuck his

nose out and beamed expectantly, Burdock agreed.

Since it was still too wet to pasture the animals, Dewey threw a little hay over the pen walls, dropped a few scant buckets of water into the pens too, and milked Mrs. Brown. Then he closed her back in her stall and headed again toward the front of the barn.

"Tug! Pull! Get ready!" he yelled over his shoulder and disappeared into the toolshed.

What Dewey did next was this:

1. He harnessed up the horses.
2. He brought them outside and hitched them to the small wagon.
3. He backed them slowly into the barn down the wide central aisle.
4. He loaded up every last scrap of the garage equipment, even stripping off the shelving and the cabinets.
5. He moved it all into the woodshed attached to the house.

"Oh my stars," said Nanny in a whisper, as she watched.

"What?" asked Burdock, noticing the sudden unease in her voice.

"Look," said Nanny.

It had not escaped the animals' detection that Dewey cared more about his antique car than just about anything. Now it became clear that he was moving his precious garage equipment.

Suddenly, any last doubts as to whether Dewey was serious about burning down the barn were gone.

And Tug and Pull were being forced to help set their own demise in motion, while the other animals watched.

"We've got to get out of here!" cried Figgy, staring at Dewey's nearly emptied-out room. All that remained was the car itself. Dewey would move that last.

"How — how's the hole coming?" asked Mrs. Brown. Her voice sounded shaky.

"Not fast enough!" cried Figgy. "I can't dig when Dewey's around. So I have to dig at night. And the ground, I'm afraid, is *hard*. The top was soft, but underneath it's much harder than I thought."

Burdock peered through the slats at the pig, whose hooves were cracked, snout chapped, and knees chafed.

"But what if Dewey sets the barn on fire *tonight*?" asked Fluff. It was a valid question.

"Huff!" puffed Figgy, heaving an exasperated sigh. "*I don't know!* I'm doing the best I can!"

"Of course you are, Figgy Piggy," said Nanny. "We'll sort it out." Even petrified, she couldn't help but be encouraging.

"Oh, don't be a ninny, Nanny! We could all be *pot roast* if I don't dig faster!" Somehow Nanny's kind words were making Figgy feel worse.

The horribleness of the situation was becoming frighteningly real.

They each tried not to think about it, to

push the thoughts as far away as possible, but everyone's imaginations betrayed them, conjuring up scenes too vivid to ignore.

The fire would start at the outside and they would have to watch the first crackles, the first smoke, as it skulked up the walls, licking the wood tentatively. They would have to watch it intensify, gaining strength and confidence, watch it begin to gorge greedily, indiscriminately, on the old boards. They would have to watch it swell and grow. Watch now as it engulfed everything. Watch its roaring. Watch its speed. Watch it hurtling toward them with a force now so out of control, it could not have stopped itself for anything, not if it wanted to. Hold this back? Never. Escape this power? Impossible. Toward them would come at last the devouring heat and flames and destructive power of such massive proportions that it would simply grind down anything and everything in its path, and that would be the end, *their* end.

That this was a real possibility was so completely palpable that it emptied out the chests of the animals, and all that remained was the low, persistent buzz of fear.

Burdock really wasn't accustomed to being overwhelmed by fear. You could say he hadn't even felt lasting fear that night as a young cat when he lost his eye. It had happened so quickly he hadn't had time to *feel* much of anything.

And in the intervening year, he'd hardened up, grown accustomed to the world around him, and was now rarely surprised, let alone afraid.

But like the other animals, fear seized Burdock now. It wrapped its cold arms around him and squeezed tight until all he could take were shallow breaths. Dewey was putting his plan into action. There was no question the barn would be coming down.

The gray cat ran to the feed room and watched the last loaded-up wagon go down the aisle.

Pull turned slightly and gave Burdock a knowing, doleful look. Burdock received Pull's warm, brown gaze and held it with his one blue eye, but then, before the horse was past, he looked away.

Leave, a voice whispered in the cat's head. *Save yourself,* it said. *Go!* it commanded.

11

Digging

With the storm over, the temperature began to drop fast. That afternoon, for the first time in a while, the sun was in the sky, but still the air was cold, almost crackly, and seemed to be headed toward freezing.

Toward midday, the animals heard Dewey drive off in the car, and Figgy started digging again.

She tried to concentrate on her work and not think about anything else. "Focus, Figgy," she said quietly to herself. "It's up to you. This is the only way we're going to get out."

It wasn't easy. She pawed and scraped and scooped, trying to find a rhythm. Fluff and Nanny and Tick stood waiting for the pig to push them dirt, and when Figgy did, nosing it through the cracks, they spread it around their pens to get rid of it. They were a good team, but the going was slow.

While he teetered over what his own plan would be, Burdock had somewhat reluctantly agreed to Nanny's suggestion; he would stand watch at the barn doors, and alert everyone the moment Dewey returned.

Mrs. Brown felt helpless. She wanted to contribute somehow, but she was on the wrong side of the aisle to help Figgy. And even if she hadn't been, she wasn't especially limber, at least not enough to go about bending her nose to the ground and pawing at piles of dirt. She looked over at the horse brothers, who were now back in their stalls, their heads leaned together, clearly discussing something.

Mrs. Brown let out a low "Hmmm." It was a sigh, but there was a musical note to it and she liked the way it sounded and she did it again, "Hummm." Her mother used to sing, back when Mrs. Brown was a calf at the McAllister farm a few towns away. Remembering how the singing always comforted and lulled her, she began to sing, very softly.

"When the moon hits the sky
like a big bale of rye, that's amore.

When the world seems to shine
like the sweat of a swine, that's amore."

Nanny leaned over the pen to listen. She was waiting for her next distribution of dirt from Figgy. "That's nice, Mrs. Brown," she said.

"Cowbells ring ting-a-ling-a-ling,
ting-a-ling-a-ling and you'll sing, 'Vita bella.'

Lambs will play tippy-tippy-tay,
tippy-tippy-tay, like a gay tarantella."

Fluff shuffled over and tried to sing along.
What she lacked in musicality she made up for
with enthusiasm.

"When the creek makes you drool
'cause it's sweet and it's cool, that's amore.

When you hoof down the street
with fresh grass at your feet, you're in love."

The words of the song went softly around and around, and after Fluff joined in so did Nanny and Tick, singing as they worked. Even Tug and Pull's full baritones came in once the brothers had stopped their talking, and Figgy dug, and dug, and dug to the regular rhythm. It helped her concentrate.

It went on for what must have been a long time and their voices and steady movements seemed to warm up the barn, or at least made it feel less cold.

Suddenly, with a squeal, Figgy exclaimed, "I see light! I'm through!" And there it was: a star of clear, bright afternoon beaming into the barn.

And then Burdock gave the signal that Dewey was back.

12

Alone

The others didn't need him anymore right now. Burdock tiptoed away to the farthest corner of the tool room, where the horse tack was kept. One of the horse blankets had fallen from its hook and Burdock padded onto it, turned around, and lay down, his body a small, gray circle.

It was strange. He hadn't realized it until now, but he'd felt a little lonely while Figgy dug and the others helped and sang. He hadn't sung. Stationed by the barn doors at the front and separated from the others by the feed and tool rooms, Burdock had felt outside of the group, removed from their unit.

He stood up to shift position, nestling in closer to the wall. Now he was all but hidden by the blankets hanging above. He closed his eye and thought back to a time when he had rested in this same spot not so very long ago. Remembering how he'd felt then, he blew out a big sigh, ruffling the long fur on his paws.

When Burdock first arrived on the farm, dumped at the Baxter farm driveway, he didn't know where he was. He wandered for some time through the fields and around the pastures until he found the house. When a heavy door opened, Burdock tried to go in.

"Whoa, where'd you come from?" said a voice and a boot pushed him back out. "No cats here."

But Burdock didn't know where else to go, and having no other plan, he stuck around. He was young but bedraggled. As he'd roamed the spring fields, Burdock had quickly become covered in horrible sticky burdock burrs that latched on to his long fur. After a week, Grady took pity on him; the farmer collected the kitchen scissors and cut away the worst of the burrs, then brought the cat up to the barn.

"*Burdock.* Not easy to get rid of. That's your name now." Grady grunted. It was hard to tell, but there might have been a hint of a smile in his voice. "Now make yourself useful. We've got mice."

Of course Burdock soon met the others in the barn. This was before Tick's arrival, but Nanny was as motherly as ever and did her best to welcome him. The others too, though a little skeptical about this cat with great patches of fur missing, were nonetheless curious about the new arrival and made an effort to be friendly.

Still, Burdock had never had much opportunity to make friends and he continued to feel like an interloper, so he mostly kept to himself. He settled into the feed room and slept a lot.

The others figured Burdock liked it that way and, unless he came to them, they usually left him alone.

Which worked out well until the day Burdock was injured.

It was an early evening and the sky was already lowering October's night curtain. Burdock was up in the orchard above the barn watching for the mice that came to feast on the sweet fallen apples.

Burdock was so absorbed with quietly stalking the mice that he failed to notice the nearly silent steps of a coyote stalking *him*.

Burdock only saw the fast-moving blur when it lunged. Immediately, he jerked to the side and though the coyote's jaws clasped down on the side of his face, it was not a firm hold. Adrenaline took over. Burdock pulled back, twisted painfully away, and deftly leapt onto a nearby apple tree trunk. He fiercely scrabbled up out of reach.

Burdock stayed the night in the branches of

that tree. His eye swelled shut. The fur on his cheek matted with blood.

Only when daylight finally came did he creep back to the barn, curl beneath the cabinet in the tool room, and sleep.

Two days went by and none of the barn animals thought much of him. After all, Burdock regularly disappeared. They didn't know about Burdock's injury or that his wound had become infected. They didn't see that he was feverish, sicker than he'd ever been.

Of course the farmers didn't think to look for the cat.

As Burdock lay there too sick to eat, listening to the animals talking and laughing, he felt, not for the first time, companionless. But this time it was different; a heavy loneliness settled in him like nothing he'd ever felt, pushing down on him like a hard stone. Though voices drifted over to him, they were not meant for him. It was the lowest he'd ever felt.

He never wanted to feel that way again.

13

Gasoline

What was supposed to be the peak weekend festival for leaf peepers had become an event of much smaller scale. All this rain, and then the storm had torn nearly all the colored leaves off the branches prematurely. Yes, there was an ocean of leaves blanketing the sidewalks and amassed in wet mounds, but that was not quite what people came from far and wide to see. The tourists made pilgrimages here to see the leaves *on* the trees, their beautiful colored cloaks bandied about by gentle breezes.

But one family didn't care. The Bell family was new to the area and thought it was wonderful, all of it — the leaves on the ground, how the bare trees against the sky looked lacy at their tops, the local crafts, and the urns of hot chocolate, coffee, and fresh cider. And the doughnuts! Don't forget Dolly Maccabee's doughnuts! These confections were famous around here and the Bells had just discovered why: each doughnut was just slightly crispy on the outside, and cakey and lightly spiced on the inside. Was that a hint of cardamom? It was hard to tell. After the first discreet bite, the whole doughnut simply vanished into your mouth.

"Oh, *mmmm!*" murmured Dr. Bell, closing his eyes right there at the doughnut stand. (And yes, he was a doctor and he knew doughnuts were bad for him, but every now and again, well, there was no real harm, was there?)

"*Mmmmm,*" echoed his wife and three children, their hands and mouths full of cider, hot chocolate, and doughnuts.

While the Bell family certainly couldn't

make up for all the missing tourists, their genuine appreciation for everything gave the people bundled in warm clothes — the people who were selling their wares or giving town tours — a much-needed boost of goodwill.

It didn't hurt either that the Bells liked spending money.

"What does Dewey want with gasoline?" asked Fluff.

That evening, Burdock had seen four five-gallon jugs of gasoline sitting in the tool room on a shelf. It was hard to miss them. The rusty red containers were lined up like beacons of doom under the hanging light bulb. Everyone was in a state of panic. Fluff looked confused.

"You don't want to know," said Burdock. But since he had told them about the gasoline, he figured he owed it to Fluff to explain.

"Gasoline is a fire accelerator."

Fluff's face still looked uncertain.

"It makes things burn faster," said Burdock.

Numerous times, the cat had seen the farmers pour gasoline on a brush pile. The way it blazed up was amazing. "If you put gasoline on a fire, in seconds it blows up to ten, twenty, maybe a hundred times its size, just like that."

Fluff opened her mouth as if to speak but no words came out.

"Has anyone considered," suggested Mrs. Brown in a soft voice, "that maybe Dewey is planning on moving us out, before he burns down the barn?"

Pull gave her a skeptical look. "To where? His bedroom?"

"I don't know," said Mrs. Brown. She had never stood up to Pull, or argued against him. But she was emboldened. For all his bristle, Dewey had a fairly gentle touch when he milked her. "We know Dewey intends to burn down the *barn*, but we can't be sure of his intentions toward *us*. As far as I know, he's never tried to hurt us."

Neither Burdock or Nanny mentioned how

Dewey had roughly shoved the cat just earlier that morning. And Burdock didn't bring up how harsh Dewey had been with Fluff the other day.

"I wonder," said Mrs. Brown, "if Dewey might save us still."

"Mmmmm." Pull grunted. "A nice thought. But highly unlikely. And honestly, Mrs. Brown, do you really want to be the one to stick around and find out?"

Well, if you put it that way, thought the cow.

The daylight was almost gone and the half moon, looking like a bowl of cream, started its ascent above the trees.

Burdock slipped out of the barn. He walked down the slight hill to the end of the driveway where the mailboxes stood askew and looked up. Beside him, dry tansy stalks rasped together.

Now there came another noise that grew steadily louder — a car engine — and lights appeared from the right. Burdock jumped back into the foliage and watched the car pass, following the glowing taillights until they disappeared around the corner.

Somehow Burdock knew that town was that way, but how far it was he had no idea. He could go down that road. He was independent and capable and he could walk a little while. He could probably find a new home for himself.

Or he could take a different kind of chance and stay.

14

Noctua

With all the animals on edge, it seemed likely they'd have immediately noticed the feeble scratching on the high window ledge, the awkward tumbling of wings, and then the soft *thump* of an object striking the ground like a clod of mud. But at first no one did. Perhaps the whirling of their own worried minds or the gallop of their own hearts consumed their attention.

Several long moments stretched out. It was cold in the barn. Too cold.

Then, finally, Fluff was alert.

"What was *that?*" she whispered.

The sheep peered nervously about in the dimness of the night barn and *Oh!* there it was — the ghost — no, the owl — that she had seen the day before, lying face up in her own pen, motionless.

"Help!" bleated Fluff, standing up abruptly and backing into a corner. "Figgy! Pull!" If a whisper can be a shout, that's what this was: "It's that owl! *IN MY PEN!*"

"The owl?" called Nanny across Figgy's pen. "Here? Well, say hello!"

Figgy had been digging quite furiously. Her body ached and the skin on her snout and front legs was like sandpaper, but she had hardly taken the time to notice. She hadn't stopped to notice anything. But for this she stopped. Panting and weary, and mantled with dirt, she trudged over to the boards and poked her snout through a crack.

Instantly she knew something was very wrong.

The owl just lay there. If Figgy knew anything about owls, it was that they were the most graceful of creatures. But one wing was inelegantly propped against the downy body; the other was outstretched in a gawky, slack position, feathers fanned like fingers. Figgy felt a pull of despair.

"What's wrong with him?" whispered Fluff.

"I don't know," said Figgy. "Go see if he's warm."

Fluff raised an eyebrow and gaped at Figgy incredulously.

"Go on!" urged Figgy. "It's just an owl. Not nearly your size."

"It looks plenty big to me," said Fluff, eyeing the still parcel of feathers.

"Come now, Fluff, don't be like that. If he were in my pen, I'd go right over." Figgy wasn't sure this was entirely true. There *was* something a little intimidating about an owl — they didn't exactly seem of this world — but this wasn't the time to admit that to Fluff. They needed to find out what was wrong.

"All right," said Fluff, drawing in a fortifying breath.

In truth, though dubious, Fluff was curious. She squared her woolly shoulders and tiptoed over. Gradually she bent her own head down to the owl's, finally touching her nose to the sleek, cream-colored feathers. She took an exploratory sniff.

Poof!

Abruptly there was an explosion of wings and a plaintive squawk.

"Baaaa!" bleated Fluff. Her head reared back and she fled to the opposite corner of the pen.

Even Figgy had stumbled back a few steps.

The owl tried to stand up, but fell back down into the hay.

"Nanny!" said Figgy, urgently but not loudly. "Can you come over here?"

"Coming," called Nanny.

Nanny hopped out of her pen and trotted around to Fluff's. The goat quickly assessed the situation. It wasn't clear if the owl was sick or injured or just exhausted, but something was very certainly the matter. Nanny cleared her throat.

"Hello," said Nanny quietly. "Hello, owl. Are you all right, dear?"

There was no answer.

"Are you hurt, love? Can we get you something?'

Again, no answer. Nanny's eyebrows drew up and together in concern.

"You needn't worry, hon, we wouldn't think of harming you."

The owl shifted just slightly in the hay. It seemed as if the dazed bird might attempt again to get up, but thought better of it.

The horses' heads angled over their stalls' half doors. Mrs. Brown stopped chewing her cud.

Seconds ticked by.

"Very — hungry," came a weak but surprisingly low, sonorous voice.

"Hungry? Oh, *love*, we can help you there!"

It seemed like such a simple solution, the goat was suddenly buoyant. She loved a fixable problem, and she turned to go raid the feed room, something she would never have imagined herself doing, but she paused and seemed to be momentarily at a loss ... "But, well, remind me, what is it an owl like you eats — ?"

"Voles! Rats! And mice, of course!" called Tug, triumphant in this piece of owl knowledge. He knew about owls from Hal, their previous handler, who hated mice and often joked about getting a pet owl.

"The owl needs a mouse!" called Tug now. He paused, then burst out, *"Burdock! Where's Burdock?"* The big horse craned his neck, leaning as far out of his stall as he was able. "Where *is* that cat?"

Just when they needed him most, the cat was gone. Maybe he was down at the house, or out prowling the night, or maybe he was just — gone. The animals looked about and called. Nanny went to search in the feed and tool rooms, and called up the stairs to the loft. Tug and Mrs. Brown exchanged uneasy glances. Pull thought back to the consuming fear he'd seen in the cat's eye when Dewey had harnessed the horses to empty out his garage.

And then, Burdock padded in.

He had been walking up the driveway, back toward the barn, and was still a little ways away when he became aware of the commotion inside. Were they calling his name? Silently, he treaded up the path and stepped inside.

"What's going on?" he asked quietly.

"Oh, *there* you are!" said Nanny, trotting over, visibly relieved.

But Nanny didn't ask where he'd been. She rushed to explain the owl situation, finishing with, "Burdock, can you catch us a mouse?"

"Can I catch a mouse?" asked Burdock. "I am a barn cat. A mouser. That is the essence of—"

"Burdock, dear! Just—please—go!" commanded Nanny, before returning to check on the owl.

Nanny thought the bird was startling to look at, even lying on its side as it now was. Not exactly beautiful, but simply exquisite, like nothing Nanny had ever seen before. The feathers all along the owl's back, head, and wings were not actually white at all. They were both tawny and brownish gray, and speckled throughout with white as if they had been lightly snowed upon. But the underside of the bird was indeed white, flecked here with tiny dots of gray. Most extraordinary of all was the face; it was truly, amazingly heart-shaped, and also white, except for a thin dark border. Into this silky valentine of down were set two closed eyes. Nanny had gotten a glimpse of the eyes, black and shiny like marbles, and she could tell immediately, those were intelligent eyes.

Burdock broke Nanny's trance. He sprang up onto the corner post of Fluff's pen, a mouse dangling from his whiskered mouth, and quickly inspected the owl. A moment later he hopped down into the hay, ran over, and dropped the mouse by the still owl's head.

The owl's eyes sprang open and spied the mouse. The owl lunged. Food at last.

Not long after the food was consumed, the owl started to recover, at least enough to sit up, run its beak over a few feathers to straighten them, and regain a kind of dignity.

Fluff, Nanny, Figgy, and Burdock gathered around and silently watched. Tug and Pull and Mrs. Brown looked on as best they could from across the aisle. Tug looked especially pleased to see the bird recover. It was gratifying that he had known what to order for dinner.

Nanny had

even agreed to let Tick out of their pen, and brought him around to watch through the openings in Fluff's. After all, Nanny reasoned, it was entirely unclear what might become of all of them tonight or after. It seemed only right that if nothing else Tick should at least get the chance to meet this glorious, winged creature.

Tick couldn't stand it any longer.

"What's his name?" he whispered.

"Shhh. We don't know, love," said Nanny as quietly as possible.

Everyone was trying to give the owl some space, but that didn't mean everyone didn't have questions.

The owl, wings combed and settled back in place, swiveled that arresting head and seemed to take stock of everyone at once. Resting its intelligent gaze briefly on the cat, the owl spoke. "Much obliged, Burdock."

How does the owl know my name? wondered Burdock.

The others glanced around at one another. They seemed to be thinking the same thing.

"Noctua," began the owl, "my name is Noctua. And I am a she-owl."

"No kidding?" whispered Fluff, unconvinced. "A *she*-owl? I thought all owls were he-owls?" She turned to Nanny for confirmation. "Are there really she-owls?"

"Of course," answered Noctua, giving her feathers a firm shake. "How do you think we get he-owls?"

Fluff thought that over.

Figgy smiled. She liked that Noctua was a female, and a tough one at that.

"What does it mean, your name — Noctua?" asked Tick.

Mrs. Brown wanted to know that too. She liked the sound of the word; it was like a phrase of a song, descending lightly down the scale — *Noc-tu-a*. But it didn't sound like a name.

"Noctua," said the owl, "is the owl constellation. My father was an amateur astronomer, so he liked to say. Really, he just appreciated stars."

"So then," continued Tick in his clear, young voice, "where did you come from? What happened to you? How did you get here? What is it like to *fly*?"

"Hush," said Nanny. "Too many questions."

"I'll tell you," said Noctua. "I have a lot to tell you."

15

To the Rescue

But before the owl could begin, she started to tremble. It was barely perceptible at first under all those feathers.

She stopped talking and seemed to disappear into herself, and the animals wondered if she intended to hold off on her story. But no, something again was *wrong*. Her feathers started to quiver and her beak clacked, but no words came out. Was she shivering?

What was happening? Was the whole barn shaking? But no, it was just the owl.

"What's wrong with her, Mama?" asked Tick in a low voice.

"I don't know," whispered Nanny, and then

a shade louder, "Noctua, dear, can you tell me what's wrong?"

"I feel — I don't feel —" The owl stopped.

"I think she's in shock," said Figgy. "She needs to get warm. She's cold." Figgy looked around for something to warm the owl.

The other animals looked around too. There was hay and rope. There were buckets for water. But there wasn't anything to wrap an owl in.

"Mama," said Tick, "What about Fluff?"

"What *about* Fluff?" Nanny asked.

"What if we warmed the owl with — Fluff?"

Nanny looked at Tick. It really was a good idea.

The problem was Fluff had been frightened by the owl and remained as far away from the bird as she could possibly be.

"Fluff," said Nanny, leaning over to speak privately to the sheep. "The owl needs your help."

"*My* help?" asked Fluff.

"She is in shock," said Nanny gently. "At least we think she is. We think that is why she is shivering. She needs to warm up. Fluff, she needs *you* to warm her up."

The sheep looked skeptically at Nanny.

"Fluff," said Nanny, "if I believed in fate, I would say Noctua was absolutely meant to land in your pen. Look at your warm, woolly coat. You are undoubtedly the best one for this job."

Fluff considered this. The thought that *she* could be the *best* one for anything was astounding and she liked how it made her feel. Important. She wasn't used to being recognized for anything particularly positive.

"So what would I have to *do*?" she asked hesitantly.

Nanny was pleased. "Just go over to her, slowly so as not to alarm her, and lie down right next to her, I think maybe behind her would be best and, well, try to get right up close so your wool is like her blanket."

Fluff followed the directions perfectly, doing just as Nanny had suggested. Gently she lowered herself down behind the owl and rolled onto her side. Then she scooched up so that the warmest part of her, her woolly stomach, was against Noctua's back, and her legs were on either side of the owl.

When the sheep's touch reached Noctua, at first the owl stiffened. She rotated her head around and fixed the sheep with her piercing black eyes. Fluff gasped and very nearly fainted. But she stayed put and the owl didn't move away.

Maybe it was clear to Noctua that she needed help and that Fluff the sheep was it.

It's hard to say exactly what happened, but the owl appeared to collapse into the sheep, allowing her feathers to melt back into the thick, cozy warmth. The sheep all but enveloped her.

It was a funny sight and if the situation weren't so grave even Nanny would have allowed herself a laugh. But this was a serious matter and Nanny, Burdock, and the others looked on in silent fascination.

Noctua stayed like that for a long while. All the animals stayed near. It was as if everything stopped. Time was suspended. Even Dewey was forgotten.

When the owl at last felt warm and well again, she gathered herself together. She stepped away from the sheep and bowed just slightly in thanks. Fluff returned to a corner of her pen near the aisle.

Nanny whispered to her now, "I think you might have just saved the owl's life."

For Fluff, it was a wondrous thought.

And now the owl was ready to tell her story.

16

Noctua's Story

"I have lived in this barn for many years," began the owl. "Longer than any of you. I remember when Mrs. Brown came; it was springtime, and that year it was a very wet spring, so wet the fields were like swamps. All the animals had to stay inside until May, and everyone was dying to get out."

"Goodness," said Mrs. Brown, somewhat astonished to have that memory back, and to know that Noctua also remembered it. "That's true!"

"And of course I remember about a year and a half ago — I believe that's right — when

Burdock arrived. He was just a young cat, and solitary I noticed, like me. Not long after that — he lost his eye."

Burdock looked up and shivered.

"A coyote, wasn't it?" asked the owl.

"That's right," said Burdock, angling his head to better take in this mysterious, omniscient creature. "All he got was my eye though."

"I know," said Noctua. "Very impressive. I've never heard of a cat escaping from a coyote."

Burdock sat up a little straighter.

"Then why have we never seen you?" asked Tug.

"I hope you don't think me unfriendly," said the owl, "but I keep to myself. It's an owl's way. I do like to listen to you all, and I hope you don't mind that I did, but I just felt most comfortable by myself. Not to mention," she continued, "I am on a different schedule from all of you. Just like my name, Noctua, suggests, I am nocturnal, which simply means 'occurring in the night.' I go out at night to get my meals and I sleep during the day."

Burdock knew that cats too are supposed to be nocturnal, but for the most part he had succumbed to a daytime schedule.

Noctua went on: "Usually by the time I leave, you are all asleep, the same when I return. That is why you've never seen me."

"I saw you yesterday!" exclaimed Fluff.

"Yesterday," said the owl, "I went out earlier than usual. I was famished. I have to eat every day but I had not eaten anything for two days because of the rain. All that wind and rain makes flying difficult. Soggy feathers are awfully heavy. We owls are not like fowl with oil in their feathers. All that wet kept me in."

"Oh dear," said Nanny.

"But finally I made a run for it. In all honesty, I didn't know what else I could do. But right away, things didn't go at all as planned."

She had everyone's attention now.

While the animals of the barn were supposed to be fretting over their possible imminent destruction, their minds were captured instead by this single ghost owl, almost one and a half feet tall, who stood off to the side in Fluff's pen. While she spun her story each of the animals settled down into the hay, or rested their heads on the wall of their pens, and felt a kind of absorbed calmness they hadn't felt since before all these worrisome days began.

Noctua proceeded with her telling.

She had flown out of the barn window early Saturday evening. That's when Fluff pointed her out to Figgy. It was darker than usual for that time of the day because of the clouds the storm had tossed up, because of the rain the clouds had thrown down. Immediately, the ferocious wind took the owl by surprise. A twisting tidal wave of air pushed back on her, overturned her equilibrium, and sucked her away like a leaf caught in a roaring river. Oh how she struggled to free herself! She beat her wings desperately, attempting to fly back at least to the barn. But the wind would not unleash her, and finally she just gave herself up to it. It marshaled her over deep woods and unfamiliar fields, past a village, over a highway, and farther, to places she had never known.

"Like a bad dream," said the owl, "the sky was full of things that didn't belong there — branches, bushes, even a chair! I prayed I would not smash into anything, and nothing would smash into me."

Finally there was a break in the storm, and the owl was released. She plummeted down, wing over wing, just managing to catch herself a little before she hit the ground and rolled under the lowest boughs of a tight grove of fir trees. It was surprisingly dry and protected from the wind under those branches. And so the owl, feeling very hungry and worn to a frazzle but grateful to be alive, puffed up her feathers for warmth and spent the remainder of the storm right there.

The dawn ushered in a beautiful, crisp day. Except for the downed trees and broken branches strewn about, there was no indication of the fury that had come before. Up from the horizon crept a warm, rosy red. The sky was clear and blue.

Noctua awoke and cautiously emerged from under her shelter. She looked around.

Below her was a slope of open land, and below that was a horse pasture, though no horses were visible. The bottom of the pasture was edged with mature maples, and through their bare branches Noctua could see a large house, smoke curling from the chimney. It was inviting, and without further thought Noctua opened her weary wings and flew down to investigate.

There was work being done to the side porch — it looked like the rotten floor was being replaced — and an electrician's van parked in the driveway.

Visible from the house, up the road a hundred yards, was a barn, a *round* barn, the kind once built with a mind toward better accommodating cows' pie-slice-shaped bodies. The doors to the barn stood open and a ladder leaned against the frame.

"A round barn," said Noctua. "I was so curious, I flew in. It was nice in there, airtight, smelled like alfalfa, the stalls were clean and the loft was very quiet. But there was not a single animal there! Not a cat, or a cow. Why keep hay in a barn with no animals? But it didn't look abandoned either; it was in too good condition."

The owl stopped talking and looked around, at Fluff, at Figgy, at Nanny and Tick, at Burdock, and finally at Tug and Pull and Mrs. Brown across the aisle.

"I know," she continued. "I know about what is going on here, with Dewey. I propose we all try to move to this new barn. It doesn't look like anyone else lives there."

"Whoa," said Tug.

"Wait," said Figgy, "before we get to that. How did you get back?"

"Oh," said Noctua, "I have a built-in sense of direction. But I was so terribly hungry now — I had not eaten for three days — so I was slow. I was flying, but just barely. It felt like my wings were weighted. I don't remember ever feeling so weak, and catching a meal was out of the question. If an owl's not quick, forget it. So I flew back here. But it took a while. I stopped to rest a few times. It must be over eight miles away, if I'm calculating correctly."

"You poor dear," said Nanny.

"Noctua," said Burdock, deciding he had something he needed to ask. "Why even bother coming back here? I mean, why not just stay at that barn, if you knew what was going to happen to this one?"

"Oh," said Noctua. "Yes, I see your point. I could have just stayed. But suffice to say, I am a creature of habit, perhaps reprehensibly so. I have lived in this barn most of my life. I have hunted in the same fields and gotten to know the trees in these woods. I know how this place smells, the sound of the creaking in these rafters, I know when to expect the spring peepers to begin and the fall crickets to end. I am used to this place and I don't like change. And I have gotten used to all of you. Even if you don't know me, I have gotten used to being here with you. If I have to move, I would like you all to come with me. Besides, I can't let you . . ." Her voice trailed off. "It would be nice to have you there," she concluded.

Nanny had installed herself on a carpet of loose hay in the aisle and was watching and listening through the slats of Fluff's pen. Now she got stiffly to her feet. It seemed as though the owl was finished speaking; Noctua had said all she was planning to say.

"Thank you, Noctua," said Nanny. "You have been very courageous. And your plan sounds promising."

"Yes, but how on earth would we *get* there?"

asked Figgy. "I don't know about the rest of you, but I can't fly eight miles."

"It does seem awfully far to walk," sighed Mrs. Brown.

"And there's no *road*?" asked Fluff.

"What if we're not welcome there?" wondered Figgy aloud.

"Honestly, everyone," said Pull, snorting hot breath through his nostrils. He had only just met this unusual winged creature, but he had a good feeling about her; he wanted to trust her. She was Noctua, the owl constellation. For centuries people had looked to the stars for guidance. Pull would never have said this out loud, but maybe the right thing to do was to follow the path she charted for them.

"We don't have many options," he said. "I mean, let's be reasonable, everyone! Who knows how welcome we'll be, but it's certainly better than here, isn't it? What else are we going to do? We can't spend the winter in the woods. We can't join the circus. Dewey isn't going to *wait* for us to find our perfect solution. This is it! Dewey has emptied out his garage! Dewey has bought *gasoline!* Don't you all see? There's really no reason Dewey won't burn down the barn tonight! If he does, I hate to break it to you, we're doomed: we can't escape now, because Figgy's hole isn't big enough yet to get Nanny out. We're trapped inside. I'm not faulting you, Figgy. I know you are working as hard as you can. I'm just laying it straight. And let's also be honest about this: even if Dewey doesn't come tonight, we sure don't have much time left. Noctua's option may be our *only* option. And except for getting there, it even sounds like a darn good one." Pull shook his head in frustration and loudly clopped a hoof on his stall door. Several of the animals jumped. The strong, steady horse had never been so riled up.

Noctua opened her wings, beat them silently, and rose up to perch on a ledge that protruded from the barn wall, over the animals' heads. She had made her offer and now she needed to separate herself just a little. Maybe she was giving them time to think. Maybe she was retreating a bit. Whichever it was, it appeared she felt more comfortable being off the ground and having the wood against her back.

Tug observed his brother. He shook his head as if to slough off any lingering doubts.

"United we stand," he said. "I'm with Pull."

"Me too!" called Fluff.

"Yay! A round barn!" cried Tick. He spun around in a circle and nearly crashed into the wall.

"Hold on now. We still have to think this through," said Nanny.

"Well, think, everybody, think!" said Figgy. "I'm going back to digging. Pull's right. Our time is running out!"

17

Working as a Team

As the hands of the village clock wound through the early hours of the night, many minds worked overtime at the Baxter farm. Everyone was on edge. When would Dewey come? All they could think about was escape. They prayed there was still time. *Dewey, don't come yet! Figgy's hole is almost done.*

As Figgy chipped and gouged away at the ground, laboriously enlarging her "escape hatch," as she now thought of it, the other animals chipped and chiseled away at a plan.

Nanny thought about whose door should

be opened first. Was there a perfect order that might buy them needed moments?

Pull thought about the wagon Dewey had used to move his equipment. If they made it until tomorrow (he swallowed hard thinking this), could the horses use the wagon to transport the other animals to the new farm? It would make all the difference if they didn't have to walk, but could *ride*. After all, even as Pull was the one to encourage the plan, he knew the journey would be easiest for him, and this made him feel guilty. Eight miles was a great distance for the others but it was not far for the big horses, and even the weight of the full wagon was negligible. But how would they get harnessed? Could they get the animals up into the wagon? And would there be a passable route through the woods, across the highway, to wherever this other barn was situated? He nudged Tug.

"Help me puzzle something out," he said quietly.

Mrs. Brown waited fearfully for the squeak of the barn doors. At this point, the sound of Dewey opening the doors could very well be a death knell. *But wait!* she thought, realizing with a start that this could be a major hitch in the animals' plan. The creak of the doors was so grating and simply so *loud* that even at the house Dewey would likely hear it when they tried to escape. Was that why he never oiled them? Was this Dewey's improvised alarm system?

But what if *they* oiled the door hinges? Could they? Mrs. Brown ruminated over this as she slowly chewed her cud.

Tick and Fluff continued to receive the small piles of dirt Figgy poked under the pen wall. As they kicked at the piles and raked hay over the top, Fluff thought about having wings. *I could really be something with wings,* she thought.

Only Burdock crept away toward the front of the barn. He needed time to think. He had spent a lot more time with the barn animals than the owl had, but she was willing to take a huge risk for them. She had traveled all the way back here, and even, it seemed, had put her life on the line to help the rest of the barn animals escape. Burdock had to agree with what Nanny had said; Noctua *was* courageous.

And here he had been thinking about slipping away alone, finding a nice, warm place for himself, and not looking back. What exactly did that make Burdock — selfish? Would leaving have made him a deserter? Or, alternately, had he just been levelheaded, prudent, *smart* even?

The cat had never been one for moral quandaries, and here he was caught up in a quandary of such mammoth proportions that he felt lost. Nothing here was straightforward. Naturally, saving yourself seemed right. Obviously, abandoning your companions seemed wrong. But what if saving yourself *meant* abandoning them?

Burdock's head felt heavy and he suddenly felt wearier than he ever remembered being.

I really don't know anything, he thought, laying his chin down onto the dusty floor and closing his eye.

But he didn't fall asleep. He found himself listening for the creak of the front door and Dewey's footsteps.

A short time later, Burdock got up and padded soundlessly down the aisle. He scaled a post fronting Figgy's pen and looked out into the near-dark barn.

Of course, no one was asleep.

The animals were pacing in circles and pawing at the ground.

Eyes roved in the darkness and ears swiveled to catch any warning sounds.

Burdock saw that Nanny had her nose up to Figgy's pen and was whispering gentle encouragements. "Thatta girl, Figgy! You are good and strong. You're almost there, Figgy Pudding!"

Figgy was working like a machine. Her hind end was in the air but her front half disappeared into the hole. She was twisted, too, as if she was trying to claw at the edges of the tunnel. And when she emerged, scooping out the dirt, Burdock saw just how badly her snout was scratched and bruised and how cracked her hooves had become. Still, Figgy kept on, digging ceaselessly.

It was then that a new feeling seeped into the gray cat; he felt an unexpected admiration for his barn mates, all of them. The feeling stung. While he had only done begrudgingly what had been asked of him, everyone else was contributing fully as best as they were able. Tick and Fluff were moving and hiding dirt. The horses and Mrs. Brown were helping to strategize. Nanny was pulling everything and everyone together, and Figgy, well, her contribution was painfully obvious. All in this together, they were working as a team to mobilize their escape.

And it was not even a sure thing — far from it! That was the part that hit Burdock the hardest. If Dewey showed up now — and he very well could — it was over. All of their work would have been for nothing.

How could Burdock have considered walking away from that?

He remembered what Pull had said a few days ago in the pasture: "You just want to believe your friends are on your side."

Burdock knew he didn't have it in him to be

courageous like Noctua, or instrumental like Nanny. And clearly, he wasn't as dedicated as Figgy.

But he *could* at least be trustworthy. That was worth something.

Burdock jumped down from the post and padded silently out of the barn. He would start by scouting out what Dewey was up to.

18

Almost Caught

The lights were on in the kitchen, but Dewey wasn't there.

The radio was on in the mudroom, but Dewey wasn't there.

The TV was on in the den, but Dewey wasn't there either. *Where was he?*

Burdock tiptoed back up the stairs, across the bathroom linoleum, and slipped out the window. The three-quarters moon was bright overhead, bright enough to give the cat a shadow that stalked him exactly, step for step, as he walked the high ridgepole to the shed.

Back on the ground, Burdock stood for a

moment and listened, his ears swiveling first to the left, then to the right. Still nothing.

This can't be good, he thought.

Burdock headed again to the barn. All of a sudden, the night seemed unnaturally quiet. The kind of quiet that suggests something shady is happening.

Burdock broke into a trot and was just coming up on the barn's east side and stepping into the light shining down from the peak when he heard a muted crunch. Instantly on guard, the cat lowered his ears, flattened his stomach to the ground, and skulked low and fast around the corner. This was the west side, Figgy's side, and — *oh!* — there was Dewey walking slowly around the periphery, now pausing, now crouching. *Yikes! Was he lighting a fire?* With all of his senses on high alert, Burdock crept cautiously closer. *No,* Burdock understood immediately. Dewey had discovered Figgy's hole and was *investigating.* In a matter of moments

Dewey would figure out that Figgy was digging from the inside.

"YEEEOOW!" Burdock delivered his loudest screeching call, added some snarling and hissing for greater impact, and tore past Dewey like a beast unhinged. The flamboyant outburst had the desired effect; a shocked Dewey lost his balance and toppled to the ground.

"Burdock! Holy meatballs! What has gotten into you?" shouted Dewey as he righted himself. "And you raccoons!" he yelled, turning to look at the darkness of the hole in the foundation. "If I catch you digging under this barn, I'm gonna shoot you!"

He called his warning loudly up into the night before stomping the rest of the way around the barn to the back entrance of the garage.

Inside the barn Figgy had stopped digging. *What in the world was that?* she wondered. Was Dewey yelling to her? Her heart pounded. She was so close to finishing the escape hole — the possibility of being caught now made her weak.

A few moments later, Burdock watched Dewey in the garage. He had a measuring tape in hand and seemed to be figuring out exactly how much space the car took up.

Once his calculations were complete, Dewey patted the car on the hood. "Good night, Baby Blue," he said, switching off the garage light. With long strides, he walked down the slope toward the house.

Burdock followed at a safe distance, watching as Dewey's silhouette went into the woodshed. The cat was careful to keep to the shadows. He tucked behind a barrel and only his eyes shifted to take in Dewey's movements as the man now measured the tight rows of stacked wood, first their length, and now their combined width.

Finally Dewey lifted his hat and scratched the back of his head. "Should work," he murmured. Then he disappeared into the house.

It wasn't hard for Burdock to figure out.

At least it looked like the animals had one more night.

Burdock stood in the moonlit driveway and watched as all the windows in the house — the kitchen, the den, the upstairs hall, and finally the bedroom — went dark.

19

The Plan

In the barn, in the predawn hours of the morning, their plan was hatched.

Nanny called a meeting and everyone attended, including Noctua, who had come back from a successful hunt and was starting to feel like herself again.

"Such good news!" said Nanny. "It's almost a new day and the barn's still here! *We're* still here!" Her face looked bright and open with relief. "And Figgy thinks the escape tunnel is just about big enough for me to squeeze through." She looked at the pig. "I don't know what we would do without you, Figgy Piggy! So you think just a few more hours of digging, right?"

"I think so," said Figgy. She was very tired and very dirty but so close to finishing, her eyes shone with anticipation.

"Wonderful!" said Nanny. "So tonight's the night."

"And just in time," said Pull.

"Oh?" said Nanny. "Why's that?"

"Go on, Burdock," said Pull. "Tell them what you told me. Tell them what you saw Dewey doing."

So Burdock explained what he had witnessed earlier that night, all of Dewey's measuring. "Seems likely Dewey's preparing to move his car to the woodshed so it won't burn down in the fire."

Figgy lifted her snout to speak. "Well, we knew he would move the car somewhere. He's just ready to do it now. Which means the fire is close."

"Right on the money," said Tug with a sigh.

Tick bungeed up and down, near to bursting.

Beside him, Nanny stood very still, considering.

"Okay then, does anyone want to put forth a motion?" she asked.

Figgy grunted. She was too tired for official proceedings.

"I will," said Pull. "I move that we, the animals of Baxter farm, relocate to the round barn."

"I concur without a shadow of a doubt," said Tug.

Nanny raised her eyebrows at the horse.

"He means he seconds the motion," translated Pull.

"Okay," said Nanny. "Are there any other motions?"

There weren't.

"Okay, then," continued Nanny, "let's vote.

All in favor of moving to the round barn say 'aye.'"

"Aye," came the resounding cries from both sides of the aisle, and from Burdock in the middle. It seemed as if everyone had spoken, though it was hard to tell with certainty.

"All against, say 'nay.'"

"Nay," mooed Mrs. Brown quietly.

"What?" cried Figgy. "Why *not?*"

Mrs. Brown looked down. She ran a long tongue over her nose and blinked her eyes. She took a step back. "I mean," she said, "nay for me. Just me. You go. I'm not going."

"Of course you're going!" cried Figgy. "Don't be a nutter! We're *all* going. The vote was just a silly formality — no offense, Nanny. Mrs. Brown, what*ever* are you thinking?"

"I," started Mrs. Brown reluctantly, "well, there's the milking. I have to be milked. But it's more than that. I, I just don't think I could walk that far. I've thought about it. My knees are bad and I'm afraid I'd slow you down, which could be dangerous for all of you." She lifted her head. "I promised myself I wouldn't hold you back. I want you all to go."

"Oh pish," said Figgy, "being a martyr is no fun. You need to rethink this."

It was quiet, and in the moments that followed Burdock sighed.

"Mrs. Brown," intoned Pull. "I am hoping you won't need to walk."

Mrs. Brown's gaze flickered and she turned toward him. There was a question in her soft brown face but she didn't speak.

"If Tug and I get harnessed again, to the wagon I mean, maybe we can manage to *stay* harnessed, and then we can pull you all there."

"Oh!" said Nanny. "That's a thought." She paused. "But why would Dewey harness you today?"

"To move the wood," chimed in Tug. "He has to move the wood out of the woodshed if he's to relocate his car there. And it's unlikely Dewey will transfer all that wood — wherever it is go-ing — without the aid of the wagon."

"And then," said Mrs. Brown, "well, I don't understand. If Dewey does hitch you up, why wouldn't he just unhitch you, like always?"

"Well, he would," jumped in Pull, "unless we can distract and befuddle him so thoroughly that he forgets."

"Distract and befuddle him — how?" asked Figgy.

"Nanny will have to let a few of you out of your pens, and when Dewey comes back to the barn with us and the wagon, you all make a break for it, go crazy, run wild, like Fluff did that day."

Fluff lifted her chin and smiled broadly.

Pull continued, "We'll have to really give him a good runaround. Wear him out and jog-gle up his thinking so much he can't tell his ear from his elbow. While that's happening, *we'll* slip into the barn all quiet-like and hope Dewey just forgets to unharness us."

"Oh! Oh!" volunteered Tick. "I can run! Let me! I can do *that!*"

"Now, Tick, love," said Nanny, "I don't know. Remember, this is not a game. This could be dangerous. Dewey will be angry and he can be unpredictable."

"Oh, let him go, Nanny," said Figgy. "Tick is quick. He might really help. It even sounds fun." She winked at Tick. Tick grinned.

"Are you in, hon?" Nanny asked Mrs. Brown gently. "We need you."

"Oh dear, my running days are long past," the cow demurred.

"No, I mean, will you *come?*" said Nanny, realizing the misunderstanding.

Mrs. Brown still wasn't sure what to say. She worried about being a burden, a millstone around the other animals' necks. She had had her life. At least most of it. She didn't want to keep others from having theirs. But then, she had to admit, the fire did sound absolutely *terrifying.*

"If it works out this way," she said cautiously, "with the wagon, then yes."

"Very good!" cried Nanny, triumphant. "And we'll find you a milker, Mrs. Brown. I have faith in that, don't you worry."

So the plan was set, Figgy would finish the escape tunnel today, and tonight would be the night.

20

Scheming

Breakfast behind him, Dewey stood in his usual coveralls and boots, and now a green woolen coat, surveying the situation again. His breath steamed the air as he stood on the porch rubbing at the scruff on his chin. The weather forecaster this morning promised the arrival of colder weather, below freezing, with a possibility of precipitation. *This just might work,* he thought.

He would have to move several rows of wood from the woodshed onto the porch. It wasn't ideal, but it would do. Grady insisted on neat even rows, but that didn't matter to Dewey. He would just make a big pile on the porch.

"Okay," he said to himself. "Let's do this."

It was just as Pull had figured. Burdock watched as Dewey harnessed the horses, attached the wagon, and started to hurl chunks of split wood into the wagon bed.

All the while, the barn animals were in a state of anxiety and excitement.

As soon as Dewey was out of the barn, Figgy of course went back to digging.

Tick dashed about in his pen, ricocheting off the walls.

"Dear boy," said Nanny, "you're going to wear yourself out. You need to save your energy for when Dewey returns." But her words had no effect. Tick was as capable of staying still as a buoy on a stormy sea.

Fluff too was wound up, still circling around

her pen, first clockwise, then counterclockwise, then clockwise again. She was grateful whenever Figgy pushed her more dirt. It gave her something to do.

Noctua was not asleep, but resting up in the rafters. She worried it was too late to retrace her route back to the round barn; she should be around in case she was needed. It wasn't that she was afraid she couldn't find the barn. She knew *she* could get there. But it was entirely different when she had to navigate a route by considering what obstacles would hinder the barn animals on the ground. She'd never had to think about crossing the landscape in this restricted way.

Mrs. Brown and Nanny were discussing the creaking door.

"Gosh, you're right, Mrs. Brown!" cried Nanny. "If Dewey hears the doors open, we're caught." It was amazing to Nanny how many things they had to take into consideration. Escape should not be taken lightly. What other things were they forgetting?

"Any idea what we could do about the creaking?" she asked.

Mrs. Brown had been thinking about that. She knew that usually a door is oiled with an oilcan, and that a few drops of WD-40 squeezed right onto the creaky hinges would do the trick. But none of the animals could manage a can's nozzle, even if they knew where to find one.

"Let's ask Burdock to look in the tool room," suggested Mrs. Brown. "See if there's anything at all that looks oily. It doesn't have to last, we just need something to quiet the creaking this one time. Then, let's hope, we're gone."

Again Burdock was summoned, only this time not from sleep. Though most of him was unmoving like a crouching statue, his gray tail flicked slowly back and forth. He had stationed himself in the doorway to await the horses' return and signal the others. He was the self-appointed sentinel.

But now he left his post and stood between the velvety brown head of Mrs. Brown and the cinnamon head of Nanny.

"What is it?" he asked.

The cow and the goat explained, ending with, "Just look for anything oily."

"Oily," said Burdock and trod quickly down the aisle to the toolshed.

The tool room was a mess. Burdock snaked between the accumulated mounds of metal and glass, looking in each open jar and pail. Most of the cans were capped but a few weren't and in one of those, not too far from the door, an oily sludge sat on top of opaque dark paint. Or that's what it looked like.

Burdock went back and reported his findings.

"Will that do?" he asked.

"I should think so," said Mrs. Brown.

What Burdock didn't tell them was that the gasoline jugs that he'd previously seen on the shelf had been moved. They now stood ready right at the edge of the door.

21

Dewey's Final Step

All morning Dewey pitched wood into the wagon, steered the horses around to the back of the house, and pitched wood off the wagon onto the porch.

Finally there was plenty of space for his Baby. Satisfied, Dewey tethered the horses to the railing and went inside for lunch.

He clomped through the mudroom and the radio announced, "below freezing." He stomped into the kitchen and the radio warned, "icing." Dewey heated up the leftover morning coffee, fried some onions and bratwurst and bread, and thought, *Perfect.*

After lunch, Dewey climbed up into the loft above the woodshed, jockeyed equipment about, and hauled down a large metal tub. He put this into the wagon and used the garden hose to fill it to the top.

Too full, really, for some of the water sloshed out as he turned the horses and wagon around and walked them down the angled driveway to the dip at the bottom.

It was here that Dewey bailed out the tub, throwing bucket after bucket of water onto the dirt drive. With the ground already nearly frozen, the water had nowhere to go; it pooled and sat. In no time it would be ice.

Three water loads later, everything was set. There was only one last thing. Dewey needed to move his car. Again, he tied the horses to the porch railing and headed for the garage.

"Here comes Dewey!" cried Burdock, standing up.

"Let's go!" said Nanny, backing up, readying to jump her pen wall and open stalls.

"No, wait, I mean, without the horses!" said Burdock.

"Wait, what?" said Figgy. "What's he doing now?"

"I don't know," called Burdock. "The horses are still at the house."

"Oh my goodness," said Mrs. Brown. "I just hate the constant *unknowing* of this all."

"Okay, wait, he's going around the side!" Burdock relayed now.

"Oh my goodness," said Mrs. Brown again. She gulped in some air.

"He must be getting the car," said Burdock. *His last preparation.*

Dewey fired up the engine and let it idle for a minute before he backed the car out of the garage and drove it slowly down the hill. His handling was deliberate, as if the vehicle were made of glass. He nosed his Baby into the narrow space he'd cleared in the woodshed, with all the practiced precision of a tailor threading a needle.

Half an hour later Baby Blue was parked in place, the woodshed was swept clean, and the radio hung on the wall from two shiny hooks. And now Dewey untied the horses from the porch rail and led them and the wagon back to the barn.

In the fading light, the barn looked almost beautiful, a dark glowing red against the indigo evening sky, and Dewey had a momentary change of heart. This barn had been here for more than a hundred years.

"Ah, never mind," he said. "Out with the old!"

He lifted the oak bar, creaked open the doors, and an explosion of legs and hooves and a curly pink tail flashed riotously by.

22

The Runaround

"*Great Scott!*" yelled Dewey, jumping back.

Tick, Figgy, and Nanny had all escaped the barn, each plunging off in different directions.

Dewey stood stunned, his arms hanging limply at his sides.

Finally he gave a thundering shout, spun around, and pounded after Tick. The chase was on.

Right behind them, Burdock raced into the grass to monitor the situation.

In no time, Tick reached the end of the driveway, zipped across the road, and scrambled through the wire fence encircling the abandoned pasture.

Soon Dewey arrived at the fence too, but as he tried to clamber over the old wire, the fence simply sagged toward him. There was no other way but for Dewey to yank up on the bottom edge, flatten down onto his stomach, and slither under.

Up ahead, Tick twisted through the pasture, avoiding the worst of the spiky plants. But Dewey had to battle the brambles and thistles with only his bare hands.

"Oh, hornets!" he yelled, emerging from the grasp of two bushes, his clothes covered with burrs.

He ripped off prickly clumps. *Where was Tick now?*

Dewey reached the edge of this pasture, where the land opened up to a hay field.

There!

Dewey crouched low and executed an awkward loping crawl on all fours. Hunkering down still lower, he pulled himself along with his elbows. Tick would never see him coming. He moved forward this way, dragging his body through the grasses, popping his head up now and then to get his reference points.

Dewey didn't register the slight thrum of a motor that had approached along the road and was idling off to his right.

It was Mrs. Chestnut, who drove the mail truck. She was craning her head out of the open door to see Dewey lying on his stomach, his clothes muddied, burrs all over. She cautiously called out to him.

"Hello, Dewey? Are you — quite — well? Do you need a doctor?" The mail mistress raised her eyebrows and quickly surveyed the empty field beyond.

"Oh, yes," said Dewey. "I mean, no. I mean, I'm fine!" He hastily jumped up and pulled down his coat.

Mrs. Chestnut eyed him.

"Are you absolutely sure?"

"Yes!" said Dewey, impatient. "Fine!"

"Okay, well, if you're sure, I'll be off then!" said Mrs. Chestnut, cranking the wheel of the old truck, and slowly accelerating down the road.

This is ridiculous, thought Dewey.

He turned back to the field, zoned in on Tick, and ran full-throttle through the thigh-high hay. A few moments later, Dewey snatched Tick with decisive force, tucked him under his arm like a football, and delivered him back to the barn.

"What rubbish!" Dewey yelled.

Slinking behind, silent chaperone to the whole escapade, Burdock thought, *A good start.*

Figgy was next. The pig was in the garden behind the house.

As soon as she saw Dewey she started capering enthusiastically about as if she were performing some complicated and lively country dance.

Burdock tiptoed into his hidden spot under the rosebush and watched. After all Figgy's digging, Burdock expected her energy to be diminished. But once Dewey was on her tail, Figgy cavorted through the cabbage plants, skipped through the corn stalks, and frisked between asparagus fronds without a hitch.

Just as Dewey came close enough to lunge for the twisted handle of her tail, she bowed under his fingers, feinted deftly to the side, and hoofed splendidly away. Dewey caught nothing but a fistful of chilled autumn air.

"Of all the CRUD!" he yelled as he lost his balance and fell into the cucumber patch.

And Figgy, after a backwards glance, went snorting and squealing away around the corner of the house. The look on her face said *delight*.

Of course Dewey still caught Figgy. Burdock knew he would. But when at last he did, she re-laxed her substantial pounds into a full deadweight, giving Dewey no choice but to clasp her around the middle and heft her up the hill like a rock.

As Dewey lugged her past Burdock peeking out now from the tall grasses, the pig gave the cat a wink.

23

Hang On, Nanny!

At last came Nanny's turn, and something had shifted. Dewey was *angry*. Burdock saw it as soon as Dewey reemerged from the barn; his face had taken on an uncomfortable shade of red and his eyes were fixed. Dewey vaulted into the pasture after Nanny, snatched up a large stick from the ground, and swung it over his head.

"Nanny!" he bellowed. "You better get back here!"

Burdock caught the frightened flash of Nanny's eyes. And they both knew: if Dewey reached Nanny he was going to *wallop* her.

What could he do? Burdock was nothing against Dewey and a stick, but Nanny needed help and he was all there was. He didn't hesitate. He shot forward, exerting his natural feline grace and speed to their fullest extent, and came right up behind Dewey. Dewey saw him, turned, and swung, narrowly missing Burdock as he rolled away. But now Dewey chased after Nanny again, and the cat realized they could both be squashed by Dewey's anger—this wasn't going to work. *But wait!*

"Hang on, Nanny!" Burdock whispered to himself. He spun around, tore back down the hill, raced through the barn doors, and swerved around the horses and wagon, now tucked into the back of the aisle.

"What's happening?" called out Figgy. But Burdock didn't have time to explain; he scrabbled around the corner and up the back stairs to the loft.

"Noctua!" he called. "Noctua! Where are you?"

One minute later in the pasture, just as it was clear that Dewey had the advantage and would finally catch Nanny, a huge white bird plunged silently between them. Talons extended, it swooped down on Dewey. With the impeccable timing an owl is known for, it seized the stick and swung it around, nearly striking Dewey.

Dewey ducked and fell. *"No wormy way!"* he cried.

Nanny saw her chance. She skirted around Dewey and pelted back to the barn.

"I don't *believe* this place!" sputtered Dewey, standing up and watching as the owl soared up and away over the trees.

Finally he stomped back to the barn and locked Nanny in. He banged the barn doors closed. He threw the bar down into the slots and stormed away.

A moment later Noctua glided in through the upper window and Burdock crept forward into the middle aisle.

Once Dewey was out of earshot, the animals looked at one another and softly cheered.

"Hooray!" cried Fluff.

"We did it!" exclaimed Tick.

"Tied a knot in *his* tail," chuckled Tug.

Nanny turned to the cat. "Thank you," she whispered.

Burdock closed his eye and sighed. Nanny was okay. As harrowing as it had been, it had *worked*. Tug and Pull were still harnessed to the wagon at the back of the aisle, the hole was dug, and everything was ready to go.

Tonight they would escape before Dewey set the barn on fire.

24

What Do We Do Now?

For a good ten minutes the barn buzzed with excitement, everyone talking about the escape and the trip, fidgeting and fretting and discussing and hoping.

Then the hinges creaked and Dewey walked in. Burdock hadn't even been keeping watch at the door. This was a shock.

"Time for your suppers! And your milking, Mrs. Brown." Dewey seemed to have calmed down but now he looked perplexed as he studied the horses and wagon at the back of the barn. "How'd you fellows get in here without me seeing? And look at you! I guess I need to unharness you too."

Given everything—his exhausting animal chase, his anger, his intentions—it seemed odd that Dewey was here, even bothering to attend to the animals. But after countless years, this daily routine was so thoroughly ingrained in the farmer that as long as the animals remained he simply couldn't *not* do it.

Dewey unharnessed the horses, hastily filled everyone's feed troughs and water buckets, and milked Mrs. Brown. He went into the toolshed and gathered an armful of tools and then he stood at the front of the barn and looked back. Tucked off to the other side, Burdock had a clear view of Dewey and couldn't help but wonder, *Does he look a little scared?* It was hard to know.

Dewey turned off the light, closed the big doors, and slid the heavy brace into the slots.

Outside, it was starting, very lightly, to snow.

There was a collective sigh inside the barn.

"Oh nooo!" moaned Figgy.

"What do we do *now?*" asked Tick.

"Now what do we do?" echoed Fluff. The sheep felt forlorn. She wished she could fill herself with air and float up, out the side window, into the sky, like a balloon.

Mrs. Brown hung her head. She closed her eyes, and though it embarrassed her, she couldn't help herself; large, silent tears seeped beneath her lashes and coursed down her soft cheeks. She turned her head away.

Slowly, Burdock looked around. Watching Mrs. Brown and Nanny, small Tick, the big horses, silly Fluff, and clever Figgy, Burdock tried to think of the right word to describe them. Maybe *friends* wasn't really quite the right one. After all, Burdock *lived* with these animals, slept and ate beside them, listened to their talk, and shared one roof every night, all year round. Maybe Noctua had been on to something. The barn animals might not be exactly like him but, he saw now, they were his real family. Burdock stood up.

"Listen," he said, trying to sound assured. "Eight miles *is* a lot. I'll be the first to admit that, but we can do it. We will walk. I have the shortest legs of any of us. But if I can do it, in this rotten cold, then you all can! Mrs. Brown too!" The ten-pound cat turned and leveled his good eye straight at the cow who, at over nine hundred pounds, weighed nearly one hundred times what he did. "Okay, Mrs. Brown?"

Figgy laughed. "That's chutzpah, Burdock! Okay, let's! What the heck?" Her voice grew louder. "Really, what have we got to lose?"

"A hill of beans!" said Tug.

"That's right," said Pull, brightening. "I agree. I'll lead the way. And Tug too. We weigh a ton. Each. And we have enormous feet, alarmingly large feet!" His voice sounded almost buoyant. He lifted his feet and crunched audibly about in his straw for emphasis. "We'll trample down a path for the rest of you!"

"I'll bring up the rear," said Nanny. "Make sure everyone is accounted for."

"Of course you will!" said Figgy. "You know,

you really do deserve a better name than Nanny. You're way beyond that."

"Okay, everyone," said the goat. "Now quickly, eat all your dinner and drink a lot of water; you're going to need it. Then, we *move!*"

25

Trying to Escape

Once dinner was hastily consumed, Nanny jumped her pen wall and worked on opening Mrs. Brown's door first. Nanny was nervous and it took her three tries, but she finally knocked the block upright and Mrs. Brown pushed out. She was free.

"Okay, go to work," said Nanny in a whisper, for suddenly everything felt tense and a cloak of near silence felt necessary. "Oil them up!"

Mrs. Brown hastened to the toolshed where Burdock pointed out the pail he'd seen earlier. The ungainly cow turned around and backed up with Burdock calling directions.

Trying to Escape

"A little bit to the right, Mrs. Brown. Turn more, yes, there you go!"

She went carefully, stepping over and around the jumbled mess, and dunked the shaggy end of her tail into the bucket. *Blech.* Greasy indeed! But she would set to work oiling the hinges while Nanny squeezed through Figgy's tunnel.

"You think that's big enough?" asked Nanny in a low voice. "Oh dear, well, it's going to *have* to be. Now if I get stuck, you'd better push me!"

Figgy had pulled all the hay back from the escape hatch and the dimmest of light shone through.

"Here I go," said Nanny. "Wish me luck." She hadn't realized until right now how frightened she was of this whole escape. Getting through the tunnel, opening the barn doors and all the stalls, sneaking away from the farm and, of course, not getting caught.

Nanny took a big breath. She crouched low, knelt down, and wriggled her head and front hooves into the hole. The ground was surprisingly cold and hard, like cement. This *was* going to be tight. She squirmed in farther and she could see a patch of outside. A few tiny snowflakes were swirling down. The crisp air actually felt good, invigorating. She pushed with her back hooves and worked her way nearly halfway through the tunnel, and managed to press in farther. *Oof, it's tight.* She tried to take a deep, fortifying breath, but the hole constricted her. And now that the thickest part of her was wedged in the hole, she couldn't get any traction; her front legs stuck straight out, and her hind hooves pushed back but caught on — *nothing.* Oh no, was she *stuck?*

Burdock's bristly head suddenly appeared.

"Oh Burdock, dear me," Nanny said not loudly. "I think I'm stuck!'

"You can't be," said Burdock. "You're almost through. Tell Figgy to push you."

Nanny twisted her head slightly and whispered insistently, "Figgy, give me a shove!"

Figgy said something, but it was muffled and

Nanny and Burdock couldn't make it out. Had Figgy understood her? Was she just stuck here? But oh — Nanny felt a push.

Inside the barn Figgy pushed, first with her head and shoulders, then she turned and shoved with her back, digging with her hooves in the dirt. It didn't seem she was making any

headway either. "Sorry!" she snorted. "I can't! It's just — it's too — it's —"

There! In a crumble of dirt and sand Figgy collapsed back into the hole and Nanny was propelled ungracefully through into the night.

"You did it!" the pig heard Burdock exclaim from the other side. "Now around to the front!"

Papery moths were flying in and out of the cool luminescence above the barn doors. Weak as the light was, Burdock didn't like the nakedness of it. He wanted the dark. Nanny looked as if she felt the same.

"Burdock," said Nanny in a hush, staying

off to the side, in the shadows. "Are the doors oiled?"

"I think so. Mrs. Brown did it. Let's hope it works."

"Okay, good," said Nanny. "Now for this lock."

Burdock watched as Nanny studied the doors and the bar that held them. He stole another glance down to the house. The kitchen light was on, but nothing else. No Dewey in sight. Smoke curled out of the chimney, a twist of gray against the black sky.

"Let's do this," whispered Nanny.

She tiptoed up to the doors and leaned her head forward, beneath the bar, until her forehead came to rest on the vertical boards. Slowly she stood up taller, hooking her horns under the bar, and tried to lift. From his position, Burdock saw the bar give. It lifted an inch, then another, and a bit more, and now Nanny stood on the tips of all four hooves, straining

her head and neck and shoulders, stretching as high as she possibly could, struggling to lift the heavy oak brace free. But it wasn't enough. The bar wasn't clearing the slots.

"Ahh." She sighed and lowered her head, and the bar slid back into place. She ducked back into the shadows.

Burdock moved closer, standing just near enough to Nanny that her coat brushed against his face. Had he never touched her hair before? It was unexpectedly soft.

"What if you try running and butting the bar off?" Burdock asked.

"Yes," said Nanny, studying the doors again. "I think that's the only other way. I was just worried that might make too much noise." In the cool air, her breath came out in warm puffs of white. Burdock looked quickly again at the farmhouse window and shivered, but Nanny kept her gaze on the doors.

Now the goat backed up a few steps, positioned the end of the bar securely in her sights, then bounded forward and bucked up in one unbroken motion.

The bar was knocked cleanly up and out of the slots, sailed through the air, and landed with a small thud in the grass off to the other side.

Stunned, she turned to gape at Burdock.

"Wow!" he whispered. "Neat! All right, now, step back. I'll tell Mrs. Brown to push open the doors." He ran quickly back into the barn.

Burdock gave the okay. Though the doors had been oiled, still he steeled himself to hear the loud, grating creak. But as Mrs. Brown nudged the wood and the doors swung out, they opened as silently as theater curtains at the start of a performance.

The overhead light filtered into the barn and all the animals leaned out of their stalls. Just like Nanny's, their eyes were bright and frightened and awed.

"Okay, we have to be quick!" said Nanny in a fervent whisper. "Once I get you out, go around to the side of the barn where it's dark. I'll be the last one, so when I arrive, we bolt!"

As Mrs. Brown had already been freed, she nodded and slipped around into the dark. Noctua left her spot on the edge of Fluff's pen and went out too.

Burdock remained by the door as watchman.

Nanny began to open stalls. Her heart was pounding away and she felt jittery, almost weak with nerves, and her first go at Pull's door was way off. The second one too.

"It's okay, Nanny," said Pull. "Steady on."

"Right," she whispered. "Steady on." She zeroed in on the block and hit it just right, and Pull touched the boards with his hoof and the stall door opened. The huge horse came out, looking at her squarely.

"You're something, Nanny," he said, and went out the barn doors past Burdock to join Mrs. Brown.

Tug was freed next, easy enough, with two tries.

"Bravo," he whispered, giving Nanny a crisp nod. He tried to pick up his hooves and set them down lightly; it wasn't easy to move two thousand pounds and make no noise.

On to the other side of the aisle. Tick's door lined up on the first try.

"Go!" she said, giving him a nudge. "Go around the side with the others. And *stay* there!"

Then Figgy. Figgy's block was looser, and Nanny had to go back and forth, tapping a bit left, a bit right, but finally Figgy was out, trotting away, calling, "Almost there, Nanny! One more!"

Now Nanny came to Fluff's pen.

Nanny lined up, bucked, and rammed the block squarely from the right.

Such a solid chop should have had an effect. But the block didn't move. Not an inch. Nanny backed up and tried again, putting more force into her assault, but though her aim was perfect, the block didn't budge. It made little sense. *When was Fluff out of her pen last?* Nanny calculated quickly. The sheep hadn't gone out when they all tried to distract Dewey, but that was because Nanny had misjudged how much time she'd need to open the gates. So then, it had been several days. Had all the rain swollen Fluff's door tight against the block?

Fluff peered anxiously at Nanny through a crack.

"It won't open?" she asked, her eyes so big you could see bands of white all the way around her pupils.

"Not yet," said Nanny, determined not to show Fluff her own fear. "Let me give it another go from the other side."

She came around, backed up, and hit the block with a mighty blow. Did the impact move it a little? It was hard to tell. She didn't think so. *How could this be?*

Nanny tried again. *Smash.* And again. Her head rang now from the solid hits, but she wouldn't give up. Goats have a reputation for being stubborn. Well, she could be a goat in this respect too. *Smash.* She was going to get Fluff out. She was angry and scared and there were tears in her eyes. How could they get this far and be defeated by one chunk of wood? One nail?

Time was ticking down and now the watchman cat seemed to detect a kind of doom. Under his fur, he felt the prickle of Dewey's imminent arrival.

Quickly Burdock turned and ran.

26

Tick

Tick knew he had been told to stay in the shadows around the side of the barn, but whatever was *taking* them so long? Where was his mother? He couldn't just *wait*. While the others talked excitedly in nervous, hushed voices, Tick had slipped back to the corner and strained to listen. All that came to him were occasional muffled *thunks*. He wanted to go back in, to see what the delay was, but he knew his mother would not approve.

Tick walked a hundred feet out from the barn and looked around at the darkened landscape, the indistinct black outlines of trees, the curving smudge of road. He looked down to the house, and the kitchen light was on. He could see a silhouette cross before the window and back. *Dewey.*

He glanced anxiously back at the barn. *What was taking them so long?*

Several icy flakes settled on Tick's nose and he shivered. *Something was wrong.*

A flicker of light made Tick look back down to the house. He could see a small bright blaze pass by the windows inside the kitchen, illuminate briefly the darkened mudroom, and disappear. Seconds later, Dewey was standing still in the woodshed doorway with what looked like a torch. *A torch.*

Tick froze. He had been told explicitly to stay beside the barn and in fact at that moment he could not move a muscle. But now as Dewey started forward, Tick realized if he did not buy them a few extra minutes — hopefully enough time for his mother and Fluff to get out — it was over. That would be the end.

As if a gunshot signaling *GO!* had exploded in his mind, Tick was off.

As fast as he had ever run, as fast as he would ever run again, Tick raced through the tall grass along the road, pelted under bushes, bounded over the dark lawn, and circled around to the house. He could not see clearly in the gloom, but he did not slow his stride. He took the risk of stumbling in a hole and breaking a leg. It did not matter. He ran.

He reached the house, skidded around the side, and came to the back lawn.

Had Dewey seen him? He didn't know.

Tick needed to make a lot of noise and fast. He spun around looking for something, anything that would do it. On the lawn were just the dry branches of a rosebush, and a stack of bushel baskets. On the back porch, an old glider swing, a broom — nothing would work! Tick was desperate. Dewey would be walking toward the barn with his torch.

Tick turned his head to the garden and a slight glint in his peripheral vision demanded his attention. Now he looked up past the porch railing and saw, marvelously, the gleam of glass. That was all it took. Tick hurdled up the three steps, put down his head, and bashed the nubs of his fledgling horns into the old window.

The noise of the shattering glass was spectacular.

Glass splintered down and flew back up in a hailstorm. Tick closed his eyes, leapt off the porch, and ran, his breath gone, his heart smashing like a hammer in his chest.

27

C'mon!

What in the world was that?

Dewey changed course and ran back around the side of the house.

The light from the torch was so bright it swallowed up the dark around him; Dewey felt blinded. He held the torch off to the side and ran as quickly as he dared, his feet sounding loud on the dirt gravel, now soft on the grass. He came to the porch and halted in his tracks. It was spooky. What in heaven's name *happened* here? Was this some kind of practical joke instigated by . . . he couldn't even imagine who. He held his torch behind him and looked out into the dark. A deer?

If he didn't have immediate plans, he would have gone for his gun right then.

Nanny backed up again when she heard footsteps come through the doors.

She stopped in her tracks.

It was Pull. Burdock was there too.

"Oh my!" She gasped. "Thank goodness it's you." She stumbled back a step.

"Let me, Nanny," said Pull. "You have done splendidly. Let me see what I can do. Fluff, hurry, go stand against the far wall."

Burdock got out of the way too and Nanny moved over beside him. She was wheezing.

They watched. There wasn't much room for the big horse to maneuver, but quickly Pull turned and, facing away from Fluff's stall, he gave a snort, pitched his weight forward, and kicked his formidable hind legs powerfully backwards.

With his two thousand pounds of muscle and bone readying to land a concentrated blow, Pull was an imposing, breathtaking beast. Never before had Burdock seen him like this. If the cat didn't know Pull, he would have run.

SMASH! Pull splintered his massive hooves into the wood of Fluff's pen. The door tore from its hinges and plowed into the ground, sending up a cloud of dirt and dust.

In a moment, the air cleared.

Fluff looked frightened, dazed, then purely delighted.

"Oh, *PULL!*" she cried. "You've *rescued* me!"

"Let's go!" said Nanny.

They dashed out, but not before there was another big crunch as Pull's dinner-plate-size hoof stomped down on one of the old gasoline jugs waiting near the door. He stumbled, accidently kicking another can, which rolled away into the grass. Burdock sprang out of the way. Pull looked back. The first rusty old can was crumpled like cardboard. Liquid seeped out.

Tick burst breathlessly from the long grass on the side of the barn and careened into Nanny, almost knocking her over.

"Where have *you* been?" She looked at him hard.

"Hurry!" said Burdock.

"C'mon!" cried Nanny, and all of them bolted around the corner into the dark.

28

Flames

A short while later, Dewey approached the barn and stared in wonder. The doors were *open*. He advanced to the barn threshold and the ground squelched. What was that? He couldn't see.

He leaned over, crouched, brought his torch down low. And caught the smell of gasoline just a moment too late.

A massive billow of fire erupted as the gasoline caught. Flames flashed across the ground like lightning and then, as the other gasoline jugs simultaneously caught, there was a thunderous explosion.

Dewey stumbled backwards, landing heavily in the dirt.

Would you look at that.

Without another thought he pushed up and ran through the arc of flames into the barn.

Dewey spun around. Where was Pull? Tug? Where were the goats, the cow, the pig, the sheep? They were not here. His shock was so great he didn't register the intense heat of the fire or its devilish roar as it blossomed around him, gorging on timber.

Dewey propelled himself out of the barn as one of the burning doors broke free from its hinges and crashed to the ground, a fizzing of sparks falling like hot molten rain.

He ran out across the road, through the tall grass, stumbled onto the lawn, and collapsed onto his knees.

Bright flakes of ash and snow glided lazily down, dusting his green coat white.

29

Through the Middle of the Night

From the top of the ridge that Noctua had brought them over, the animals looked down into the valley and saw the barn burning. The snow was coming down thicker now and against the white sky the glowing red was dazzling, brilliant, ethereal.

They had turned at the sound of the explosion and now stood and watched awed as the fire grew and grew, engulfing the barn in mere minutes. Even from this distance, they could see the roof buckle and split and collapse into the red maw of fire.

No one knew what to say. They had escaped. They were safe. That had been their home. They were alive. It was gone. It was all so strange, nothing felt right.

Burdock shrugged his fur and the cold coating of snow he had collected slid off.

Minutes went by, and finally Figgy said, gently, "Let's go, shall we?"

"Yes," said Nanny. "Noctua, would you please lead on?"

Noctua flew ahead, scouting out fences, houses, steep descents, obstacles of any kind, and then flew back, flapping her wings for Pull to follow. It was a challenge to find routes without barriers or bodies of water, to find ways across roads with impossibly high banks.

Pull kept his eyes to the sky, while stomping his feet through underbrush and branches, crushing down brambles and steering the clearest path under Noctua's wings.

After Pull came Tug doing the same, trampling and clearing, and offering encouragement, then Figgy, Fluff, Mrs. Brown, Burdock, Tick, and Nanny.

It was a sight to see — this long line of animals walking bravely through the woods.

As they walked, Nanny asked Tick where he had been before they all converged at the side of the barn, and Tick told her everything: about Dewey, the torch, the window. Nanny was staggered to realize her son had disobeyed her and by doing so had probably saved them all.

"My pet," she said. "My wonderful, fearless Tick."

But besides that, no one talked much, except to say things like, "Watch this branch!" "Mind that hole!" "Mrs. Brown, you're going to have to duck here!" and so on, and they fell into a kind of rhythm, through woods, across fields, down hollows.

The group stopped several times to rest, mostly for Mrs. Brown. But really, she was

doing surprisingly well. She was keeping up. Perhaps having just *survived* was fueling her adrenaline, and though her knees felt stiff and her hips were sore she didn't complain once. Anything was better than that fire.

There were however a few minutes of panic as they were crossing a ridge, when Fluff stepped down awkwardly and seemed to just tumble away into the dark.

"Fluff! Where's Fluff?" cried out Mrs. Brown in dismay. One moment the sheep had been right there in front of her and then, just as suddenly, she was gone.

But Noctua quickly found her at the bottom of the hill and Tug came to stamp a path for her and before long they were back on their way.

"I'm certainly awake now!" exclaimed Fluff.

"That'll do it every time," laughed Figgy.

Up front, Noctua circled around again and called a warning to Pull, "You'll have to head to the right here and then look for me and I'll lead you back on track. Don't get fenced in."

Mrs. Brown heard that and the song came easily, naturally, awakened from her memory and her mother long ago. As she stepped through the snow, she started to sing.

"Oh, give me land, lots of land
under starry skies above.

Don't fence me in.

Let me eat of the sweet
open pasture that I love.

Don't fence me in."

Besides the chuff of feet on snow-covered grass, and the crackle of snapping twigs, Mrs. Brown's voice was the only sound. It started wavery and low but through the dark trees of the shadowy forest it was cheering, fortifying. First Fluff joined in, then Nanny, trying to follow along.

"Let me be with my friends
in the evenin' breeze

and slumber in the shade
of the cottonwood trees.

Send me off forever but I beg you please

don't fence me in."

Now came the others, the horses' deep har-
monies adding a warm texture, and a kind of
solidity, to the voices. Burdock had never sung
before, but he joined in with his gravelly voice.
It made him forget about the cold.

As a chorus, the song bound them, confirmed
that though they might feel cold and adrift and
uncertain, stepping down onto frozen foreign
ground, traveling through the middle of night,
at least they were together. They each felt infi-
nitely better for having the others near.

"I want to gaze at the ridge
where the west commences

and graze on the grasses till I lose my senses.

I can't look at hobbles
and I can't stand fences.

Don't fence me in."

Mrs. Brown thought there was a verse missing there, but it didn't matter, it was enough, and they sang it over and over, round and round, up hills and down, as the snow came down thicker and settled on the backs of the horses and the sheep, like a thin blanket of pure, white cotton.

The first snow of the year made for slippery roads, so Gavin Henry, the town librarian, was driving slowly and carefully down Highway 81, not above thirty miles an hour. He squirted his windshield with wiper fluid to clear the snow and squinted out. Before him, crossing the road into the trees on the other side, was that —? No! It sure looked like a milk cow, a cat, a kid goat, and a nanny goat, all in a line. Gavin pressed gently on the brake and leaned forward over the steering wheel. A *goat?* It was gone now. He reached over for his now-cold coffee and took a large gulp. He needed to stop eating so much sugar . . . He would tell no one about this.

The animals came over the last ridge in the dark early hours of the morning. They had been walking for more than nine hours. Their singing had stopped a long time ago and now they just trudged, heads down, each following the tail of the animal in front. Only Pull kept his head up, looking always for the owl who flew forward and back, beckoning the horse this way or that with a tilt of her wings. She was glad he was large and dark; it made him easier to find in the snow. He was glad she was there charting him through the trees, this unfamiliar white night landscape.

Finally, Noctua flew down and rested on a branch of a tree just ahead. Pull came to a stop beside her. Noctua had recognized the grove of trees she had sheltered under during the storm. They were on the edge of the woods, at the top of a slope. This was it.

"You can't see it now in the dark and with this snow, but the barn," she said to Pull, "it's just down there."

"Wow," he answered. "You did it. *Thank you.*" He took a breath. "Okay. Let's go."

30

Arrival

Before the sun came up, the animals settled into the round barn. The doors were not locked and Tug easily nudged them open. Inside it was dry and warm with soft hay to lie on and to eat.

Like voyagers across an ocean, the animals felt they had arrived at a new shore, solid land. With hardly a word, they crept in and lay down, not in individual stalls, but in the big open space, side by side, nose resting on back, head against hip. Once they were settled, only Noctua flew off, in search of food. She would return soon and roost in the rafters.

Figgy was next to Nanny, and after the pig had closed her eyes, she opened them again to look closely at the goat. "It's you who pulled this all together," she whispered. "Without you it would never have happened. From now on I'm calling you Gloria."

"Gosh," said Nanny, "thank you. But it wasn't just me. We *all* did it. *You* dug us out. How about I call you Figgy the Formidable? Or Madame Muscles? Maybe just Gutsie?"

Figgy snorted. "Figgy will do. Good night, Gloria."

"Good night, Figgy."

Nearby, Burdock settled down next to Pull and the weary horse cocked his head to one side and asked quietly, "You thought about leaving on your own, didn't you?"

How had he known?

"I, well, yes, I did," answered Burdock honestly. "I really didn't know what to do."

"Quite understandable," said Pull. "I would have considered escaping too if I could have. Not that I actually think I would have. But I certainly would have considered it."

"Really?" asked Burdock, looking up to meet the great horse's warm brown eyes with his one blue one. "So you don't think that makes me — terrible — for thinking about it?"

"Of course not," said Pull. "It's animal nature. No one wants to die. *Especially* not like that." He paused before adding, "Still, I'm sure glad you stayed. We needed you. You were the one who figured out how to open the stall doors. You kept Dewey from seeing Figgy's hole. You caught the mouse for Noctua. You got Mrs. Brown to agree to come, and Nanny says that you saved her. I don't think any of us would have made it here without you."

The tired gray cat didn't answer, but in the dark he moved a bit closer to Pull, gave a great sigh, and then a small rumbly purr started up like a motor.

The snow fell thickly through the dawn, covering up the animals' tracks.

In the morning, despite the snow, the Bell family's hired man, Stanley, showed up for his first day of work. He wasn't going to let the snow thwart him. He couldn't wait to get started on the Bells' projects: the stone walls

they wanted built, the chicken house, fixing the fences so they could have a few cows. Dr. Bell even wanted bat boxes, said he'd read that bats kept down mosquitoes. It was exactly the kind of job Stanley was hoping to find, and he felt fortunate. The Bell family was new to town and eager and he liked them all. They might not know what they were doing, but they'd figure it out.

Stanley walked into the barn with his coffee, stamped the snow off his boots, and stopped. Seven sleeping animals were nestled in the hay. And now out of the dim early light, a one-eyed, brambly gray cat appeared, stretched his body long and looked intently at him.

Were the Bells surprising him? Stanley laughed. "Those Bells sure are funny. Keepers, I think." He reached down and ran a kind hand over the cat.

"You want some cream?" he asked. "Me too." He lifted his coffee cup. "And if I know anything, that cow needs milking." He nodded at Mrs. Brown.

"This is good," he said to the barn. "A new beginning. Let's find a pail."

31

Home

Soon the Bell family was up, the three children dashing about looking for their winter pants and warmest boots. *It had snowed!* The first snow! They couldn't wait to go out in it.

Dr. Bell and his wife got ready too. They also were excited to see their new place dressed in winter.

Finally all the scarves and mittens were found, the laces tied and coats zipped, and the family of five stepped out onto the porch.

"Morning!" called Stanley as he came out of the barn. He was heading toward them with a pail.

"Morning, Stanley!" Jane Bell called back. "It snowed! Hey, whatcha got there?"

"Fresh milk!" cried Stanley. "From your cow!"

Jane Bell looked at her husband. And he looked at her. Each expected to see a contained smile on the other's face, a tiny reveal of the surprise they'd kept hidden. But neither of them saw that.

Stanley saw their bewildered expressions too, and suddenly wondered— But no! How could the animals have just *arrived* here out of nowhere in a snowstorm?

"Uh, better come see," he said, turning back to the barn.

Stanley pulled open a door and held it for the family. The Bells tromped in, and there were the animals, munching hay, sucking up water from the buckets Stanley had filled for them, swishing their tails, and breathing their sweet, warm breath. They were real and alive, and in the Bells' own barn. The sheep let out a low *"Baaaah!"* by way of hello.

"Look!" laughed Henry, the six-year-old, taking his mother's hand.

"Oh, Daddy! Thank you!" cried May, throwing her arms around Dr. Bell's substantial waist. *"Ohmigosh! Look! There's a baby goat!"* This was way better than any snow.

"Wow," breathed Helena, the oldest. She was transfixed, staring at Tug and Pull. "They are *beautiful.*"

"Dear?" asked Jane Bell. "Did you . . . ?"

Dr. Bell shook his head slightly, a confused smile on his face.

"They're for us, Daddy?" asked Helena. "We're keeping them, right?"

"If we can," said Dr. Bell, smoothing his beard, "then we most certainly will."

The Bells thought about putting an ad in the local gazette: FOUND ANIMALS. But no matter how they considered wording it, it sounded ludicrous. People would think they were crazy.

They decided just to listen to the local news,

read the papers, and check the town bulletin boards regularly, and if they heard anything about missing animals, they would follow up. They didn't want to steal anyone's animals, but they hoped not to lose them. Right away it had felt like the animals belonged there.

First days and then weeks went by, and the Bells became part of the town framework. They learned the history of the area from Noreen Claussen, the town clerk. They got to know everyone as they filled up their tank at Gus's Gas. And they found out where to buy Dolly Maccabee's famous doughnuts, once even bumping into the lady herself, which was a little like meeting a celebrity.

But the Bells never did hear anything about the animals; not one mention ever came up. It was as if the animals had dropped from the sky with the snow.

"This place is so cool," said May, leaning over the edge of her bunk to talk to Helena below. Tonight they realized that they'd had the animals a whole month. *They were staying.* "I mean, I thought I'd like it here. But I didn't expect to like it *this* much!"

"Me either," said Helena, looking up from her journal. At the bottom of her bed was curled a one-eyed cat, reveling in the choicest warm spot ever. "Who'd have guessed?"

And Dewey? What happened to Dewey?

The town fire truck couldn't get up the farm's driveway with a sheet of sheer ice at the bottom, and the barn burned to the ground.

But the insurance company did not rule it an accident. Not when the investigators discovered a suspicious gasoline can — the one that Pull had kicked into the tall grass off to the side of the barn. Further investigation led to the conclusion of "suspected arson." Which meant Dewey didn't get a cent.

So what did Dewey do? He rented out the house to the recently married Rosie Carmine and her husband. They loved the lay of the land here, the sloping fields, the trees, and they hoped to buy the place one day.

And Dewey left. He packed a few bags, drained his bank account, and took his Baby Blue on a tour of the South. He might be nearing forty years old, but he still had a lot to find out about himself. Maybe he'd look for Grady. Maybe he wouldn't. What he'd do next was anyone's bet.

Life at the Bell farm was more certain. The Bells and the farm animals fell into a happy daily routine. They watched the land collect layer upon layer of snow until spring arrived on the farm.

And there, in the late evenings and into the night, an owl flies low over the old horse pastures and fields. Like the owl constellation she was named after, you might not always see her outline in the darkening sky, but you can trust that she is up there among the stars, keeping careful watch.

Acknowledgments

I have had the idea in my head for a while now that writing a children's novel would be something I would like to try. I have always loved middle grade novels — these are the first books I read that made a big impression on me — and I have always loved putting together words and worlds.

But the idea of writing a novel and actually doing it are far apart, and I wasn't sure how to fill in that gap. How would I begin? Where was I going? Would I recognize the right turns? Like a snail in a maze I set off.

Despite all the solitary time I spent on this endeavor, it was only with the guidance of my family, friends, and publishing team that I made it where I was going.

I want to thank my mother, Gretchen Bond, not only for being one of my first readers, but for reading to me throughout my childhood and even beyond. I am quite sure I owe my love of books to her. Thank you to my sister, Jessica Bond, for reading this piecemeal, and whose avid correspondence on the project made it even more fun to work on. Thank you to my family in all but blood: Reeve Lindbergh, Lizzy Lindenberg, Susannah Brown, and Connie Hoffman for their careful perusal of various drafts and their valuable advice along the way. I took a lot of these suggestions, sometimes folding them into the story as if they had been mine all along.

I also want to thank a lovely cast of young readers: Walker Harris, Claire Walko, Malia

Chung, Thea Chung, and Melanie Williams for reading a nearly finished book and giving me hope that this story might actually appeal to my intended audience. Their ideas and enthusiasm helped me more than I can say.

And of course this book would never have happened without a barn-load of help from the good people of Houghton Mifflin Harcourt. Thank you to Jenny Williams and Amy Cherrix for reading with gusto, to Karen Walsh and Kate Greene for advocating for this book, to Mary Magrisso for shepherding it along, and to Megan Gendell and Alison Miller for combing the pages for errors. Thank you to Rachel Newborn for the very fine design, to Chloe Foster for finessing the layouts, and to Diane Varone in Production for seeing that this came off the presses looking like a real book.

Finally, I want to thank Ann Rider for being the thoughtful and kind editor I so needed: one who encouraged this project from the beginning, who wisely and gently pushed me to explore ways to make it better, and who reminded me constantly that above all I had to listen to and trust my instincts. Thank you, Ann.